Build Me Up

CAITLIN KLASSEN

Dedication

Some of the most incredible people are made up of a million broken pieces.

This book is for us.

Wildflowers grow, unapologetically, without asking permission from the world around it.
We, as humans, should be more like wildflowers
You know... *grow unapologetically.*

Authors Note

W hitney will forever be one of my favorite characters to create because there are many parts of myself in her. As someone who has spent different points of her life feeling less than worthy and hiding behind a smile, this one definitely was healing for me.

Similar to me, Whitney often tries to face things on her own, but throughout the book she learns how important her found family truly is and that it's okay to talk about the things she's lived through without feeling like a burden.

To those who have dealt with a difficult relationship, whether with a parent, sibling, romantic relationship and beyond, you owe them nothing and I hope you flourish in spite of them.

To anyone who has ever been abused in one way or another, *I am so sorry.* I hope that you have an April, Scout, Wyatt, or Ellie to lean on and I hope that there are wildflowers scattered throughout your life in some way or another.

It's not your fault, you didn't deserve it, and you are, and always have been, good enough.

This novel contains heavy topics of the following nature: physical abuse including hitting, throwing, slapping, verbal abuse, sexual abuse and emotional abuse.

Other matters discussed in this book that could be triggering to readers include: generational trauma, death threats, cigarette burning, scars, sexual assault (discussed but not showcased), suicide attempt (discussed but not showcased), drug and alcohol use (discussed and showcased) and open door sex scenes.

Read at your own discretion and comfort level. I am in no way wanting to romanticize or glorify abuse. Protect *your* mental health.

Please note that *Build Me Up* is Book Two in The Foundation Series, each book is interconnected but can be read as a stand-alone.

With love, Caitlin Klassen

The Foundation Series Playlist

T he Foundation Series full playlist is available on Spotify, but here are Whitney and Wyatt's top five songs.

Whitney

    1. *Yours* - Russel Dickerson

    2. *You All Over Me* - Taylor Swift and Marren Morris

    3. *Not Ready To Make Nice* - The Chicks

    4. *Humble And Kind* - Tim McGraw

    5. *A Life That's Good* - Lennon & Maisy

Wyatt

    1. *Tough* - Dylan Scott

2. *My Girl* - Dylan Scott

3. *There Goes My Everything* - Kane Brown

4. *Can't Have Mine (Find You a Girl)* - Dylan Scott

5. *Die A Happy Man* - Thomas Rhett

Prologue

WHITNEY - ELEVEN YEARS AGO

"Please be home, please be home," I whimper under my breath, wiping blood from my face as I sprint down the long driveway towards the only place that has ever felt safe to me.

I bang on the door with all my might, crying out for April to open up. The bright yellow door usually acts as a source of happiness, a moment of joy. But today it does nothing to ease my pain. I wrap my arms around my body, wincing in pain as I try to ignore the stabbing in my sides.

What do broken ribs feel like?

I don't know what I did wrong this time . . . I don't know why she lets him hurt me too. I thought things would be different after she was arrested again, that maybe this man would be more of a father figure to me.

Or protect me from *her.*

I thought things would change . . . I always think things will change.

The front door swings open and April's grandmother takes me into her arms with a gentle movement, as April approaches in the hallway. "Oh child, I'm so sorry. Let's get you cleaned up."

Like always her voice is warm and her hugs are full of love.

"I didn't know where else to go, I couldn't stay there . . ." I stare down at the ground, letting my hair shield my face. My nose continues to bleed, and I watch as it lands onto the floor.

Drip. Drip. Splat.

"I promise I'll clean it up, I'm so sorry," I whisper quickly, sniffling.

My best friend April clings to my arm, "Grandma we need to help her, I can't watch this keep happening over and over again. There has to be a way." Her dark eyes fill with tears as she leans into me.

We move towards the kitchen, April on one side of me, her grandmother on the other: a protective force field around me. Like clockwork, April's grandmother—known as Scout to April and I—places me on the counter beside the sink and slowly starts to tend to my cuts and the fresh cigarette burns lining my wrists.

I take in the bright kitchen, fixating on the vase of fresh wildflowers on the farmhouse kitchen table as she presses a tissue into my hand. I press it against my nose, wincing at the pain.

"This is the worst I've ever seen you," April mumbles, trying to keep a brave face for me, but fresh tears are pooling in her eyes.

"What happened, Whitney?" Scout asks, wetting a cloth.

My shoulders sag as I try to process what brought me here.

"It all happened so fast, I was minding my own business playing in the backyard but apparently I was too loud," I whisper as April brushes my pale blond hair out of my face. "I don't even know his name. They've been dating for a week. I'd known they were drinking, but I didn't realize they were high too. Mama just stood there laughing and egging him on."

I finally allow myself to look at Scout, the only true mother figure I've ever known, and as tears fall from my eyes again, I whisper, "Please let me move here, please keep me away from them. I'll be good and keep my head down. I'll stay out of your way, *I promise.*"

I press a new tissue to my nose, the previous one completely soaked through.

Scout sighs heavily and sadness fills her blue eyes. "Whitney, I would love for you to be with me all the time, but last time you stayed here past dark I thought they were going to skip town with you. I've tried to talk to child services, but it never gets me anywhere. But I promise you this: when you're sixteen we can try and get you emancipated, we'll find a good lawyer. They won't be able to argue with the law. You'll be free of them, and you'll have a home here."

That's three years from now—three years too long.

What if I can't make it until then?

"Mama called me a burden again; told me she wished I was never born. Sometimes I wish I wasn't born too." I blink back tears.

Focus on the wildflowers, Whitney. Focus on their beauty that blooms without asking permission.

"Why am I so impossible to love?"

April's lip trembles. "Whitney, you're the easiest person to love and I wouldn't know what to do if you weren't in my life. You will always be my sister and I will be here for you, no matter what. We'll figure something out."

Scout hugs me tight against her chest. "Me too, Whitney. We'll figure it out, but for now I think we should make some cinnamon pancakes, and then we can go check on the horses."

A small smile spreads across my face. The easiest way to pretend everything is okay is by getting lost in the small moments of joy that come from this place.

"Now . . . who wants to grab the bowls for me?" Scout asks, lifting me down from the counter.

April and I scatter towards the pantry in a flurry of squeals.

A smile spreads across my face until I feel the blood running down my lips and onto the floor in front of me.

Drip. Drip. Splat.

My mothers voice echoes in my head, like always.

Poor, pathetic Whitney.

Chapter 1

WHITNEY- PRESENT DAY

The sound of beeping machines and hushed voices fill my ears and the blanket covering my body is making my skin itch.

At least you're safe, right?

The anxious whispers of my two best friends overpowers the ringing in my ears.

I know what happened, I know where I am.

Trying to open my eyes as much as I can, I'm barely able to make out anything with how swollen my face is. I try to force a smile as I turn to face Ellie and April.

"I just wanted a girl's day . . ." I joke, my voice scratchy, but neither of them laugh, and I can only assume they aren't smiling.

It's never been this bad before. I don't need to see their expressions to know that they won't let me go home—that no amount of reassurance I give will be enough this time.

"Not funny," April whimpers, and I hear her sniffle.

A single tear escapes from my eyes, falling down my cheek.

"I'll go tell the nurses you're finally awake," Ellie says, her usually chipper voice is hollow.

Finally awake? How long was I out?

April and I have been best friends since elementary school. She and I grew up in similar home lives and we're bonded for life because of it. She was luckier than me though, in her own twisted way. Her grandma, Jean Louise Green, took custody of her after her parents skipped town when she was only seven. I spent a lot of time at her grandma's farm, riding horses, sewing, and learning what true parental guidance and love was.

She's hoping to make it big in the Nashville music scene as a singer, and in the last few months she's been starting to get noticed.

A lump forms in my throat.

Did I make her miss out on any of her gigs? Did Ellie miss work because of me?

I hope not. . .

Ellie and I met through April a few years back, when she was renovating April's house. She's five-foot-nothing and has a big attitude but is the hardest working person I've ever met. She became family to me quickly, after I learned how protective and loyal she was.

The nurses and doctor come to speak to me but all I hear is white noise. All I see is him on top of me, choking me, burning me, hitting me, throwing me, while she watches and laughs.

I hate her so much; I wish I could erase her from my life.

I will never forgive her for this one.

He almost killed me. He would have killed me if the neighbors hadn't seen and called the police. It doesn't matter that he was drunk and high. It doesn't matter because she's my mother. She should have protected me.

From who? Which time?

Focus on the fucking wildflowers, Whitney . . .

My eyes are slits, nearly swollen shut, preventing me from seeing the extent of the assault on my body, but I think that's for the best. I feel a sharp pain everywhere as April squeezes my hand. I know she feels responsible, they both do. I never wanted my life to be like this, never wanted my friends to suffer because I suffered, but pride has gotten in the way every time.

I should have known better.

The sound of April's heavy sigh slips through my thoughts, so I turn to her as she says, "You're not going back, you're moving in with me and Kyle and we'll figure out a plan. We're talking to the police this time, Whitney. I don't care what you say. We can't protect her; she doesn't deserve to be protected. I'm done letting you figure things out on your own. I'm done." Her voice is firm as her thumb traces the outline of one of the many cigarette burn scars on my arm.

She's right, and I can't believe it took me this long to finally agree with her.

All I can muster is a soft, "Okay," as tears start to fall from my eyes.

A gentle knock sounds on the door and a woman dressed in uniform steps into the hospital room, with a comforting smile. "Good morning ,Whitney, my name is Samantha, I work with the Nashville Police, I was hoping I could ask you a few questions."

"She was conscious this afternoon, but she's been out cold for hours." April's face falls into a frown. "It's barely been an hour since she woke up . . . she's not ready."

Samantha takes a cautious step into the room, reading April's body language.

"April, you called them. She's here, it's okay," I remind her gently, knowing that part of her fear is having to re-hear what happened to me.

She's been pacing the room ever since Ellie got called away to work fifteen minutes ago, which is an obvious sign that she's internally freaking out . . . and I'm trying not to fall into my own panic that's trying to rise to the surface again.

"Ms. Harris, I know this is a difficult topic and I'm sure your memory might be foggy, so if you need a break at any point, just let me know."

April sits down in the chair next to me with an apprehensive sigh. "We appreciate you coming, I'm hoping we can start by saying if this goes to court . . . we don't want Whitney on the stand, or present at all if we can avoid that."

I flash the police officer an apologetic expression for April talking on my behalf. "April is right, I don't want to testify in court, especially if my neighbors are willing to. For me, the goal is to get a restraining order if possible, and to get as far away from her as possible." I try to speak with confidence, but my voice wavers, causing April to all but force a water cup in my face.

"We can take our time . . ." Samantha reassures us, but I don't miss the way her eyes linger on April.

"She told me everything . . . I can just reiterate it?" April offers, anxiety consuming her voice.

I reach my hand out to her, giving her hand a squeeze when it lands in mine. "I'd like to speak," I say, my voice staying steady. "I'd like to tell my side of the story."

"Where is the goddamn money, Whitney?" my mom screams, slapping me across the face, causing me to stagger backwards.

I hold my hands up trying to defend myself from her fingers clawing at my skin, but her movement is relentless.

"I gave you your money last week mama, I don't get paid until tomorrow!" I try to step back, but the pile of garbage scattering our kitchen floor causes me to stumble. I shift, trying to navigate myself away from her.

"When are you going to stop being a fucking hostess? Get back with Deacon so he can give me a discount on the drugs. Just use protection, I would hate for you to get knocked up with a deadbeat daughter." She takes a swig from her bottle of vodka before placing it on the coffee table. "I sure wish I'd used protection with your waste of a father," she adds for good measure.

I bite my inner cheek until it bleeds. The thought of Deacon is enough to make my skin crawl. This is hell, but that was worse . . .

The front door bursts open and Carl waltzes in with a slimy smile, a beer bottle in his hand.

"Whitney owes me money," my mom says, pulling out a pack of cigarettes before lighting one for herself. I try to move away from them, get to my room, but Carl is large and quick to wrap his hand around my arm, slamming me into the wall.

"Pay up, bitch," he spits out. "Stop taking advantage of your mother's kindness."

"C-Carl, I did. Last week. I don't have any money left . . . I swear. Please." I widen my eyes, silently pleading with him even though I know he won't let up. He never does. "I'm still paying off her med—"

I can't finish my words before he's choking me.

"Don't lie to me. Cigarette," he commands my mom, while I try to squirm out of his grasp.

My mom approaches me. "Bad girls get punished, Whitney. I thought you would know better by now." And then she places the cigarette on my inner wrist. I exhale, trying not to cry or scream. That makes it worse for me. They prey on my weakness. She moves the cigarette up my arm as Carl continues to hold my neck with a sick smile on his face.

Once she's content with the burning, she motions for Carl to toss me onto the ground. I land onto the sticky floor as they both kick at my sides. With each kick, I feel a sharp pain growing in my ribs

"Get up!" Carl shouts but I don't move—my ribs feel broken. He grabs me, throwing me into the front door. I grab for the door handle and open the front door, hoping to make a run for it but he lunges for my leg, and I fall onto the concrete. A loud crack sounds from my arm, and it takes everything in me not to scream out in pain. Carl gets on top of me and punches my face, blood fills my nose but it's my mother's voice that breaks me into a million pieces.

"Get her out of my life, Carl. I don't care what happens to her. Never have, never will."

". . . and he continued beating me until the police showed up. I don't really remember much after as everything went black soon after the ambulance arrived . . ." I finish, coughing out my last words, while April wipes tears from her eyes and Samantha writes down my account.

A lump forms in my throat when Samantha speaks. "I am so sorry all that happened, Whitney. If you're not aware . . . it sometimes takes months or years for cases like this to go to court, but I can guarantee that we will put a restraining order in place. If you're okay with it, I'll invite the social worker into the room, and we can go over our next steps.

I nod, trying to ignore the nagging pain in my body and my desperate need for sleep again.

The next thirty minutes go by in slow motion and by the time Samantha and the social worker leave, I don't know how to process anything.

"Well . . ." April clears her throat from beside me, a sullen expression on her face. "It's better than nothing."

But is it enough?

Carl is already being held, and the likelihood of him being let out on bail is low. Apparently having a few previous run-ins with the cops and being wanted for an armed robbery worked in my favor.

But until things can be settled in court, the best we can do is put a restraining order in place and remove me as the payee for my mom's finances.

At least I don't need to pay for her medical bills anymore.

I bite the side of my cheek, numbness consuming me.

"Whit . . ." April turns to face me. "W-what can I do?"

I let my hair shield my face, hiding me from the world. Right now, I can't find the wildflowers. Right now, I want to run as far away as possible. But I need to act brave, I need to fake it until I'm okay.

"I'm tired, April, just let me sleep. Please," I say, evenly, closing my eyes to try and stop the fresh batch of tears trying to escape.

I'm fine, everything is fine.

Chapter 2

WHITNEY

It's been three weeks since I was released from the hospital, and I'm finally feeling more like myself; although I still flinch at loud noises, and I still triple check to make sure the doors and windows are locked every night. I still have nightmares about Carl and my mom.

April and Kyle have been so kind, letting me stay with them, but I'm going stir crazy and I think they are too. Kyle is the perfect match for April, he's charming and protective and he understood that she and I have a bond that nobody could ever break.

If I had my way I'd be on the farm with Scout, living a simple life but nothing seems to work in my favor. April's grandma ended up dying two months before my sixteenth birthday; two months before I met Deacon at a field party.

I was young and stupid, so I moved in with a guy I hardly knew, who promised me a way out from my mother—a safe haven. I didn't care that he was ten years older than me and an even bigger alcoholic than my mother, I thought being away from her was going to fix me.

But instead, it broke me more. He used me as his punching bag and convinced me that that was what love was—pain.

I stayed with him until I was twenty-two out of fear. He'd threatened to end my life, or his, more than a few times if I left him. No matter how many times April tried to get me out of there, I didn't want her help . . . didn't want her to get caught up in everything. But coming home to him in bed with two girls the same week my mom was diagnosed with stage one lung cancer was the final breaking point.

I had a life plan. I was on my way to finishing my Business Administration Degree when my mom got sick, and I had to drop out of college with less than a semester to go. All of my savings had to go towards her treatment, her meds, and her appointments, because she was unemployed and couldn't afford it. I remember the day she looked me in the eye and said, "You don't want to be the reason your mom dies, do you?"

She was convinced it was my job as her daughter to sacrifice everything for her, and she spent my whole life convincing me of that too.

Not like she ever made much sacrifice for me.

She wasn't dying, they caught it early enough and the tumor was small, which, as a lifelong smoker, was "impressive" as the doctors had said. Regardless, the care cost many thousands of dollars and I was suddenly in a hell of a lot of debt and back living in the place I so desperately wanted to escape.

It didn't take long for me to realize she was milking it for all she could, but I knew better than to test her. I feel the scars on my inner wrists and my stomach every day. Bruises heal quick, bottles are easy to clean up, but ten-year-old me got to learn that cigarette burns hurt and the emotional scars they leave never go away.

My mom felt better after a year and a half of treatments. But when the cancer was in remission, she decided she had a bad heart or had back pain or anything that would make the doctors click their pen and give her a prescription for whatever she could get. And when they stopped giving her medication, she went back to drinking and turned to Deacon for drugs.

Shortly after a DUI she met Carl in AA and things only got worse for me. She would say that Carl made her life do a one-eighty, but I like to say he made her do a "twenty-four." You know, twenty-four shots of tequila, twenty-four cans of beer, twenty-four cigarettes a day.

Twenty-four new bruises for me ...

She never thanked me for helping her, holding her, driving her everywhere, sitting by her bedside. Giving up my future for her.

I'd hoped cancer would change her, but it just made her twice as mean and twice as ungrateful.

Part of me hoped she would die. I know how terrible that sounds, but I just wanted to be able to say she was dead, instead of saying she was strung out on heroin.

Instead of showing up to her naked on the front porch for all the neighbors to gawk at.

It would have been easier for me.

But now I'm here, trying to find my footing and failing miserably.

I feel like I've overstayed my welcome and keep offering to go stay at a hotel but if there's anything that my best friend is, it's persistent and stubborn. And Kyle knows better than to argue with her.

I don't know how to act; I don't know how to deal with people caring for me day and night. I wish that this could be easier for me to understand and accept, but even though April is my best friend, and she has helped me through one thing after another, I don't feel like I deserve the love and support that I'm receiving.

No matter how many times April reassures me, I will always hear my mom's voice in my head.

You'll never be worth it, Whitney. You're a waste of a person, and my biggest regret.

It was a relief to be able to get back to work, but having Ellie and April rotate between being my ride to and from work makes me feel like a teenager with a curfew.

Except I'm a twenty-four year old hostess at a strip club still paying off the debt I accumulated because of my mom's medical bills.

April watches me in the mirror today while I get ready for work. Her dark brown eyes and dark features make me look more pale than usual with my sunken eyes and sullen expression. My clothes hold no color to them, everything about me feels mute these days. The only thing that shines on me is the bright red lipstick to distract from the mass amounts of foundation and concealer hiding my still fading bruises.

At least my cast is off now.

"Whitney . . ." she hums out, leaning against the door frame.

I pull my long blond hair into a ponytail and meet her eyes. "April, don't. Please don't bring up therapy right now. Or Ellie offering me a job. *Again.*"

I'm not a charity case.

"I don't think the strip club is the best place for you to be right now."

"I understand that, but I think you and Ellie have done far more than you should in order to help me."

She shakes her head, grabbing my arm as I go to pass her. "I'm just worried you're going to snap . . . or spiral. You've barely said a word about what happened since you got out of the hospital. You haven't cried since you got here. I'm just trying to figure out where your head is right now. If you won't talk to me or Ellie, then you should talk to someone else."

I don't tell her I'm fine, I don't tell her to not worry, instead I move past her and say. "I don't want to be late." I falter in the doorway, reminding myself to not shut her out completely, "Good luck at your gig tonight . . . Sing your heart out, rockstar."

I hated my job at the strip club, long before my mom's boyfriend, Carl, decided to beat me to a pulp. But now every time a slimy man tries to pay his way into the bar, or tries to squeeze my ass it makes me want to throw up more than usual. And my misery is showing. I'm getting less tips and my manager has been mostly giving me daytime shifts or making me stay longer than needed at the end of the night.

Like I needed another punishment?

Ellie has offered to hire me as an office administrator at her business multiple times over the last few years, but ultimately had to hire someone else. But the day of my accident, they gave notice. April and Ellie have tried to spin it as "being a sign," or "Scout sending me a wildflower from heaven," but I refuse to hear it. I worry that if I step into the role, I'll forget everything I learned in school and let Ellie down.

I'm worried that she'll be another person who grows to resent me for not being good enough.

I'll never be good enough at anything.

So, for now I fake a smile and continue to stand here, wishing I could fade away.

Tuesdays are slow. Kiki, one of my coworkers, is currently playing tonsil hockey with one of our bouncers. And the early September air is holding a chill tonight, making my short skirt and crop top feel even skimpier than normal.

Glenn, the manager of the club comes outside, a cigarette in hand.

My fingers fall to my most recent scar on my wrist. *I hate cigarettes.*

"Hi, Whitney." He gives me a curt nod. He's the epitome of the cliche strip club owner—middle-aged man with greased back hair, a tacky button up shirt, chain around his neck, and pants that are far too tight for his beer belly.

"Hi." I try to force a smile, but it doesn't quite make it on my face. I used to be so good at this—acting like this job was the best thing since sliced bread. But now when I look at Glenn all I see is the man who threatened to fire me for missing too many shifts. And when I told him I was in the hospital, beaten to a pulp, he'd just grunted like I'd told him a boring story.

"You used to be the best employee, Whitney—such a team player. Always bringing in the most tips. Which is impressive since you've always left your clothes on." He puffs on his cigarette, talking loudly as I let a group of people into the bar. "You need to smile more."

I fight every urge to roll my eyes.

"I will work on the enthusiasm, Glenn," I deadpan, clenching my fists, my fingernails digging into my skin.

He grunts. "Or maybe you can find another place to mope around before I start losing business."

I snap my eyes to his and all the anger and hatred I've been holding inside starts to crack.

Why am I still allowing myself to be stuck in this environment? It's not helping me. . . it's just a connection to the world I want to leave behind.

Maybe April was right, maybe I should let my emotions out.

Maybe if I can't find the wildflowers then I need to create them.

Maybe it's time to move forward.

I start taking my headset off. "Ya know what, Glenn? That's a great fucking idea. Best one I've heard in a while. I quit."

I move into the bar before he can respond, slipping through bodies grinding together until I get to the employee locker room. I empty my locker into my bag quickly, stuffing my tips into my wallet before texting April.

Whitney: I just quit my job. I'm going to walk home. I need to clear my head.

April: I'll have a cheesy movie queued and waiting for you when you get here.

Whitney: Is it too late to make chocolate chip cookies?

April: Never. Not by Scout's account!

Glenn calls out to me as I move past him in the entryway, but I don't hear him. I give Kiki a salute before I move down the street. Even with my six-inch heels, I feel like I have a pep in my step for the first time since the attack. Maybe this is just another push for me to get my life together.

Maybe this will be the best decision of my life.

Chapter 3

WYATT

It's hot as shit today, but I don't care. We've officially started on a new property and I'm eager to knock some walls down.

Almost three months ago, my boss and best friend, Scott Woods, was offered a duo home renovation show called *From the Ground Up* alongside his long-time "competition" Elenor Elm, who just so happens to be the girl he loves something fierce.

I'm not much of a romance reader, but I'd imagine there's many novels out there about forced proximity making people realize their feelings. It sure worked for them!

Either way, it was one of the best things to happen for all of us. Having TV publicity is bringing us more business now and we've unofficially joined forces in all projects. I wouldn't be surprised if we'll do an official merge at some point. Scott and Ellie whisper about business plans a lot.

Our current property is located in an older part of Nashville, with big bay windows and beams in the kitchen, but the interior is a total gut job. I've come to love seeing Ellie and Scott mix styles—he steers towards dark and classic, whereas Ellie tends to do light and bright. But the one thing they never fight over, is our trademark front door color. The one Ellie got custom made for the first property we worked on.

Having the best of both worlds has elevated our team all the more.

"Alright team!" Ellie bounces up and down in front of us. "Cameras will be here soon, but I just wanted to remind everyone that we'll be celebrating Scott's birthday tonight at his place, so bring your bathing suit and your appetite!"

I nudge Grant's shoulder beside me. He had been Ellie's right-hand man, and I was Scott's when we first met. Now the two of us are second in command together and great friends. "Are you coming tonight?"

He nods. "Yeah. We got a babysitter, so you can't harass my wife for more dirt about me, without me present."

I chuckle. Ellie had brought Grant's wife, Bree, to a night out once and I spent all night buying her wine and getting her to tell me all about Grant's most embarrassing moments.

"If anything, I can tell you all of her embarrassing moments this time around."

"I have no remorse for my actions." I smirk as the sound of truck doors slamming comes from behind us. "And no offense, but I don't see her as someone who would have embarrassing moments. She seems to have her shit together."

"Ask her about our first date, you might change your mind," he says, putting his hard hat on as the front door opens and the filming crew walks inside.

"Okay guys and gals, time to get mic'd up!" Scott calls out, excitedly. Ellie puts on the bright red hardhat Scott had bought her with the words "the most infuriating woman in the world" written on the side.

Ellie wears it as a badge of honor even though she's one of the sweetest humans I know. Seeing the two of them so happy and having inside jokes makes me crave a relationship.

It's not that I haven't dated anyone, I just never seem to find anyone who is the right fit for me. I want someone who craves simplicity and can understand the importance of found family, but also loves my mom and brother like family. My mom and Wesley mean everything to me so I couldn't imagine being with someone who doesn't get along with them.

We spend the better part of the morning breaking down walls and getting rid of the water damaged flooring in the house. My muscles are burning in the best way by mid-afternoon.

Scott and I carry the old drywall out to the dumpster in the front yard. "Are you feeling older and wiser yet?" I tease him.

"None the wiser. But listen, I wanted to talk to you." Scott takes his work gloves off, his expression suddenly serious.

"What's up? Ellie kicking you to the curb already?" I lean against the dumpster, trying to read his expression.

"Very funny, but no. Ellie has a friend that went through something. Ellie is hoping to convince her to come tonight." He frowns before continuing, "She was the reason Ellie has missed a bit more work than usual. It's been a lot for her and she's kind of shut down. I figured you might be a good person to keep an eye on her. Ellie and her other friends are pretty worried."

My brain flickers back to when Ellie missed almost a week of work during our first property and how her usually bright personality seemed dull, and how she wasn't as sassy to Scott.

I start to piece it together. Ellie having "off-site meetings" and coming back to work the next day looking completely lost . . . Scott skipping guys' night because he had a headache. I should have seen it, should have been more observant.

"Sorry I didn't realize sooner . . ." I tell Scott and his frown returns.

"Wyatt, it's not your job to keep tabs on everything. We were keeping it private. Trust me, I would have come to you sooner. You know that." He gives me a look he hasn't given me in years. "She's had a pretty rough life . . ."

I swallow. A bit of a rough life . . . *like the life I had?* I hope not. But as his words settle into my heart, I can't help but think, *at least my suffering ended six years ago.*

"Thanks for telling me." A silent question plays on my lips.

He pats my shoulder. "Don't worry man. I haven't mentioned anything to Ellie about your childhood. I just imagine her friend may appreciate another person who understands, but hasn't gotten a front row seat to her suffering."

"Is her friend doing okay now?" I ask, stuffing my hands in my pocket.

"Honestly, I'm not sure . . . She quit her job the other day and Ellie spent last night baking with her . . . which is apparently a coping mechanism. I've had way too many cookies over the last few weeks," Scott says with an awkward laugh. But hearing that she enjoys baking as a coping mechanism reminds me of someone else I know. I don't want to think about that right now though.

"From what I've heard, she likes to suppress her emotions and put on a brave face." Scott exhales, running his hand through his hair.

I nod. I know that feeling well. I didn't talk about anything until I moved out and even then, only my closest friends know that part of me.

The broken version of me.

Chapter 4

WHITNEY

"You have to come to Scott's party, please!" Ellie says from the end of the guest bed I'm currently curled up in. I've returned to wallowing today and Ellie and April won't even do me the courtesy of letting me do it in peace.

Her brown eyes are pleading. Scott is Ellie's long-time crush—try seven years of pretending to hate him—turned boyfriend, and I know I'm adding unneeded stress to her life by pouting.

"Paige will be there . . . Grant and Bree too," Ellie prompts, readjusting the purple jean jacket she's wearing. "They all really miss you."

I give her a side eye. She knows I miss them too, but I haven't wanted to see them since my attack. It might be pride or shame, but I just don't want to see *that* look in their eyes. The look that makes me feel pitied.

"If you come, we can go to the sewing class tomorrow . . ." April offers, knowing that sewing always softens my heart.

I still shake my head though. "I'll ruin your night."

Ellie huffs. "No, Whit, you could never ruin our night. We are worried about you and think a little time outside with friends will be good for you."

I close my eyes and curl into my pillow. *Maybe I can go for an hour and then leave?*

April nudges my arm. "Come on, you might just have fun. Don't make me offer to bring you to a bookstore or riding too . . . I'm not above pulling out all the stops. It's time you did something fun."

"It's a safe space, Whit. Everyone there is a safe space, I promise. I will stay pressed against your hip all night if that's what you want." Ellie's words cause me to open my eyes.

One of the best parts of Ellie is she would never lie to me or put me in an environment that would unsettle me, and if she tells me she's willing to be glued to my side, she means it.

A playful smile crosses her lips as she clasps her hands together in a pleading manner. "I'm also not above bribery." She winks at April before turning her gaze back to me. "I didn't want it to come to this . . . but I'll let you do my make-up and my hair."

I can't help but half smile. Ellie rarely wears makeup since she spends most of her day in dust and grime. But I love doing makeup and hair. Many years of covering bruises, paired with needing to look the part at the club has made me a master of disguise.

Just do it. You owe her for how much time she's taken off work . . .
And how much effort she's put into helping you heal.

"Okay, fine. Don't expect me to have a good time though," I mumble, getting off the bed at a snail's pace.

April drags me towards my closet and the two of them pull out a few outfits. Most of my clothes are still at my mom's house and I can arrange for a day to pick things up with my lawyer, but I'm not ready to go back there yet.

The girls convince me to wear a light purple, long-sleeved dress that is covered with black wildflowers. It's one of my favorite dresses. April opts to put on a purple outfit as well, so we all match. Since the three of us are all only children, the two of them seem to push the matching outfits to fulfill our "sisterhood." Normally I find it endearing, tonight I'm barely able to fake a smile.

I sit in front of Ellie, with a variety of makeup items on the counter beside us. I tell her to close her eyes as I place a light layer of pink eyeshadow on her eyelids. I keep it simple, adding a pink hue of lip gloss to her lips and some blush to accentuate her already high cheekbones.

"Perfect," I say when I'm done.

She looks in the mirror and smiles widely. "I love it, Whit! Thank you!"

Her smile is contagious, and a piece of my wall falls down.

"Oh wow! Look at that, she still smiles!" Ellie exclaims, winking at April as she clutches her heart. "Thank goodness."

I let out a humph before grabbing a tube of lipstick off the vanity for myself.

April and I each put light makeup on ourselves too, before I braid Ellie and April's hair. A life skill Scout taught me that April was never able to master . . . but sometimes I think she asks me to do it, to feel connected to Scout in her own way.

After brushing my long blonde hair into a messy braid, the three of us head into the living room. Kyle takes our photo before we move to the front door, all of them happily chatting away. I try my best to smile and act like I'm ready to face the night ahead of me.

But as we pass the mirror in the front hallway my mom's voice trickles into my head.

Still trying to play dress up? No one will ever see your beauty, because you have none for them to see.

When we pull up in front of Scott's house, my eyes widen. It's a beautiful home, but it's also a new environment for me and that makes me nervous.

April holds my hand tightly as we walk up the driveway. I replay the names of the people here who I know and love. *Ellie. April. Kyle. Paige. Bree. Grant. Mal.*

It's a safe space.

Ellie leads us up the side of the house into his backyard.

"Wow, this yard is incredible," April whispers against my shoulder.

I fake a nod even though my eyes are scanning all the faces I don't recognize. All the people with alcohol in their hands.

At least nobody is smoking.

As we near the deck overlooking the pool, Scott's laughter isn't hard to miss. It forces my eyes towards where he stands, but instead of finding his face, my eyes land on soft caramel-colored eyes and my stomach flip flops as the person's lips curve into a smile that fills his entire face—like he's never been so happy to see someone in his entire life.

I pull on my sleeves as self-consciousness fills my body.

A pretty dress won't hide your scars.

"Ellie, there you are!" Scott beams as we approach.

My eyes bounce back to the guy right beside him. He's tall with dirty blonde hair and his eyes are still staring right at me. And I'm staring right back.

I'm usually uneasy with new people–especially men, but most of me feels calm—like my heartbeat slowed down to allow me to catch my breath.

I've never seen such a nice smile before.

"Gosh baby girl, you look beautiful!" Scott gushes, drawing my attention back to him, hugging Ellie. "All of you do!"

"Scott," Ellie kisses his cheek, "This is Kyle, April's husband." She motions between us and the guy beside Scott. "And this is Whitney and April."

"Nice to see you again, Scott. In need of some more cookies?" April gives him a pat on the back, while I chew the inside of my cheek. How do I say thank you to someone for not complaining with how much time Ellie spends around me? How do I thank someone for setting up video cameras at April's as a precaution?

Scott lets out a long laugh. "Hi, April. You know I'm always down to eat." His eyes land on mine and he gives a genuine smile. "Hey, Whitney. I'm glad you came."

I nod, fighting every urge to look down and sink into the background.

Ellie motions at the other guy. "And this is Wyatt."

Wyatt.

I've heard Ellie and Paige talk about him for months—about how he was a gentle giant who could charm the parts out of a toaster. And from the weird flutter in my stomach right now, I have no doubt he could. But that doesn't mean my walls will come down.

The smile on his lips reaches his eyes again as he steps towards me.

"Hi," he says, his voice gentle even though he towers over me. "I'm Wyatt." He extends his hand towards me. My initial thought is to hesitate, but Ellie catches my eye.

She won't let anything happen to me.

I let my eyes trail down his body as I shake his large, calloused hand. He's wearing a white T-shirt tucked into blue jeans and a backward baseball hat on. He's handsome, but I know better than to trust someone just because they're easy on the eyes.

"I'm Whitney," I offer, as if he didn't just hear my name a minute ago.

"Nice to meet you."

I take his hand and continue to shake his hand awkwardly, before pulling it away. "Nice to meet you too."

Someone calls Wyatt's name, and it allows me to slip away towards April and Ellie.

"You good?" April asks, nudging my shoulder.

I let myself take in my surroundings before answering. "Yeah. I think so."

I stay close to the campfire with April and Paige for a while before I slip inside to find the bathroom.

I have to admit that getting out of the house has gone better than expected for me, but once I get out of the bathroom, I jump at the sight of Wyatt facing the sink in the kitchen.

He looks over his shoulder, turning the water off, his expression shifting as he sees me take a step back. "Hey, Whitney. Sorry. I didn't mean to startle you."

"It's o-okay." I shrug, trying to keep my tone even as I say, "You just caught me off guard."

He looks towards the countertop and back at me with a pensive look, as if he's trying to figure something out.

"What?" I ask, following his gaze to the bar.

"Can I get you a drink or something?" He tilts his head towards the array of bottles on the counter.

I purse my lips together, shaking my head. "No thank you, I don't really drink."

"Not even water?" he asks, flashing me a boyish grin.

A small laugh slips out of me, but I still don't move towards him.

"I drink water, yes."

"Can I get you water then?"

I chew on my inner cheek before replying. "Sure." Uncertainty fills my voice as I tug on my sleeve.

The sound of the back door opening makes me jump back a step but my body calms at the sight of Paige.

Paige, Ellie, and Bree are a package deal and somewhere along the line, I became the fourth corner of the friendship square. Paige is the unhinged, dye-her-hair-crazy-colors, do-your own-thing friend, whereas Bree is quiet, soft spoken and the mama bear of the group.

Paige's eyes dart between Wyatt and I. "Hey, chica, Scott wanted to know if you wanted something on the barbie." She finishes it off with a terrible Australian accent.

"Uh, yeah, sure," I mumble, moving towards her, trying to hold in my laugh.

Wyatt extends a glass of water in our direction as we go to pass, as if he's not sure who to give it to. "Here."

"Th-thanks." I take it with shaky hands, before following Paige outside.

Paige links her arm through mine, "Wyatt is cute, huh? I tell him all the time that he has the best smile in all of Tennessee."

"Yeah," I whisper, staring down at my cup, hesitantly.

He didn't roofie you, Jesus.

"You want to know the best part about him?" Paige offers, taking my cup from my hand, a knowing look on her face as she takes a sip.

"W-what?" I give her a half smile as she hands my cup back.

She smirks as we sit beside Ellie by the fire. "He'd never try to hurt anyone. He's the most gentle man I've ever met and he's respectful."

Ellie flashes me a reassuring smile. "Are we talking about Wyatt?"

"Paige is," I reply, flicking my eyes towards the patio, where Wyatt now stands talking to Scott and Grant.

"He's a good guy, Whit," Ellie says, matter-of-factly.

"I'm not ready to date," I say, looking up at the stars.

Ellie's hand lands on mine. "I know. I'm just saying if you're ever looking for a new friend or two, he's a good option. That man wouldn't hurt a fly."

I know they mean well, and they believe it, but a part of my brain can't fight the reality.

I've heard that before about other men, and every single time it's been a lie.

Chapter 5

WYATT

After we're all full of hotdogs and hamburgers, Scott sets up his speaker system and laughter fills the backyard as people dance around to the music. I'm jumping around beside Grant and Paige when I notice Whitney is sitting on the porch swing alone.

I move towards her slowly, not wanting to startle her again.

I wasn't expecting her to be so hauntingly beautiful, but when she walked into the backyard earlier, I had to clench my jaw together to ensure it didn't hang open.

Her long legs are one thing, but her green doe eyes were another thing all together.

I'm not one for the whole "love at first sight" cliche, but I have a sneaking suspicion I'll never find another set of eyes that captivate me more.

Her eyes shift towards me as I approach and she sits up a bit taller, as if she's on high alert. Something I'm all too familiar with myself .

. . but I hate knowing that she's uncertain of me because for a split second it makes me feel like I'm like *him*.

"Hey."

I keep my voice light as I push the memory of my father out of my head. "Hey. Did you want some company?"

She shrugs so I grab a nearby chair and sit close enough that I don't have to yell, but far enough that I'm not in her space or making her uncomfortable.

"Are you having a nice time?" I ask her, watching as her hands fidget with her sleeves.

She nods slowly, her eyes scanning over the dance floor. I see the brunette she and Ellie came with, giving her a reassuring smile. "Y-yeah. You?"

"Yeah, I love nights like this—hanging out with people who feel like family to me."

We both watch everyone dancing around for a moment before I ask, "Do you not dance?"

Her hand tightens around the side of the arm rest. "I do, just not tonight." Her voice shifts slightly, before she lets out a long breath.

"That's fair. So, how do you know Ellie?"

Her shoulders seem to relax. "I met her through April a few years ago. She redid a few rooms at April's house, and they clicked instantly. The first time I met her we went camping and ended up hiking up a mountain without the other girls. She became one of my best friends that day."

I take note of how her eyes sparkle, as if she's replaying her first encounter with Ellie. "Oh, definitely. She's a sweetheart. Anyone who can deal with Scott deserves a gold medal."

A giggle slips out of her mouth and a smile spreads across her face again.

Gosh, she's got a nice laugh.

And that smile . . .

"Have you worked with Scott since he started his contracting business?"

"Yeah, pretty much. He's a great boss and a loyal friend." It's my time to smile and replay the day I met him. "We met when I was seventeen and he helped me land on my feet."

Whitney blinks, as if she's trying to read between the lines.

If only she knew the condition he found me in.

I shift in the chair, trying to figure out what else to say to her.

She looks towards the dancing, and I notice her feet are tapping along to the song. "I wouldn't expect you to be such a good dancer."

"Why not?" I ask, slightly amused but also flattered that she was watching me.

Her eyes lock onto mine, as if she's trying to search my soul. "You're a contractor, right? You aren't supposed to have enough free time to have fun or have hobbies. All work and no play?"

I chuckle, shaking my head, "I'm not married to my job the way Scott and Ellie are. Also I was a Boy Scout, we were forced to learn all sorts of life skills and hobbies."

"Oh fun. Did you get all your badges?" She gives me a small smile.

"Sure did! I could probably pitch a tent with one hand tied behind my back," I joke but a flicker of something shows up on her face and I know I've struck a nerve.

Maybe she wanted to join Girl Scouts and never got a chance to?

Whitney stands up quickly, backing away from me. "I'm feeling warm. I think I'm going to take a walk around the field."

Okay . . . maybe that isn't the issue then.

I don't want to upset her more, so I let her move down the steps before saying, "Sure. No worries. I have to head out anyway, I have an early day tomorrow." It's hard not to smile at the idea of seeing my mom and my brother tomorrow.

"It was nice to meet you," Whitney says quietly, tugging on her sleeves again as she moves in the opposite direction.

"You too," I reply, giving her a slight wave before heading towards the group to say goodbye to everybody else.

"Thanks for hosting a great party, like always!" I tell Scott.

"Ellie did most of the handiwork for me," Scott replies, hugging me. "Tell your Ma, I say hi. Wes too!"

"Of course, man. Will do," I promise him, before turning to hug Ellie. "You may want to check on Whitney."

She looks around the space, an anxious expression on her face. "Where is she?"

"She went towards the field."

"Thanks, Wyatt." Her feet are already propelling her forward, as she throws a wave over her shoulder at me. "See ya Monday."

I hesitate to leave, especially knowing whatever caused Whitney to walk away is my own fault.

Scott shrugs at me. "Go home, Wyatt. She's in good hands."

I spend my drive home trying to make sense of what I said that made a wall visibly go up.

Maybe she had a bad camping experience?

I can't help but wonder why someone would hurt a girl like Whitney, she has a familiar air about her–as if we're cut from the same cloth. Scott didn't say who hurt her or if the attack was a one-time thing or a lifelong thing, but all I know is you can't always judge a book by its cover.

I know that better than anyone else.

Chapter 6

WHITNEY

I walk towards a patch of wildflowers at the back of Scott's property, sitting down in the long grass as tears threaten to fall out of my eyes for the first time in weeks. Now is not the time to relive suppressed memories . . . or break down.

I know I should go to therapy—I should have been going from the minute I was born, but I'm stubborn and I don't want to open up old wounds.

Like Deacon tying me up and . . .

I let my thoughts trail off as I search the stars, letting my fingers run along a flower. "Enough of that. Other people have it worse," I whisper to myself. My inner voice adding, *at least you had a roof over your head.*

"Whitney?" I turn towards the voice. Ellie is walking towards me with a worried expression on her face. She sits on the ground in front of me, crossing her legs. "What are you doing way over here?"

"Thinking," I say, solemnly.

"Okay, penny for your thoughts?"

I blink up at the stars, pushing all the memories of Deacon out of my head, but my thoughts can all be summed up to be the words that slip from my mouth next. "I should probably go to therapy . . ."

Her hand finds mine, as she softly says, "Probably."

I let out a loud laugh that echoes across the field. "Gee, not even a fake 'you don't need it'?"

Ellie gives me a look, one that warns me she's about to get personal with me.

I close my eyes, whispering, "What?"

"I think it could be good for you. I had to go to a few sessions because you almost died, Whit. My brain and heart shattered; so I cannot pretend to imagine how . . . loud and scary your brain must feel sometimes." A single tear slips from her eyes before she wipes it away, "I've always been the strong friend, the one who could deal with anything without it knocking me down . . . but I've never felt so helpless in my life. I know you want to solve everything on your own, but I can't sit around watching you stay in the darkness."

Sighing, I grab her into a hug and before I know it, tears start to trickle out.

"Hey, she smiles *and* cries, in one night! We're making progress!" Ellie teases, running a finger across my cheek.

I wipe my eyes as silent tears continue to flow out of me, against my will. "God, I'm weak."

"You're not weak for needing help, you're not weak for crying," Ellie tells me firmly. "And you sure as heck aren't weak for leaning on people as you heal."

My mothers voice echoes in my head, *nobody likes a crybaby.*

She picks a wildflower, placing it in my hand. "Look, I know you've spent so much of your life thinking you have to do it alone, but you don't. We are all here for you. *We* are your *family,* Whitney."

I let her words sink in, looking up at the stars. "Yeah, well . . . *she* was supposed to be my family too." My voice breaks as I say the words that I've felt for most of my life.

"I know," Ellie whispers. "It's her loss. She'll never know how selfless you are, or how beautiful your soul is. *She* doesn't deserve you for a daughter . . . and you sure as hell deserve a better mom. A better *everything*."

I lean against her shoulder, both of us letting the heaviness hang over our heads. Finally, when I find words, I hug her tightly against me. "Okay. It's time for me to go to therapy."

"It'll be tough, but I believe in you. April and I will be here with you every step of the way. I love you, lady."

"Love you, Ellie." I lock eyes with her. I rarely say it out loud to anyone but April, so she knows how powerful it is.

The room feels clinical, too white. And the clock is ticking loudly, making me want to bolt for the exit.

Maybe it's just nerves.

The office door opens, and an older woman walks in with a friendly smile, sitting on the chair across from me, "Good morning, Whitney. My name is Doctor Hilary Boate. It's nice to meet you."

"Hi," I mumble, barely looking up.

"My job is to listen, to assess . . . to provide a safe space for you." She twirls a pen in her fingers before placing it on the table beside her. "I'm sure this experience is scary for you and that's okay. I'm hoping with each session we can help build trust. You lead and I will follow at whatever pace you need."

I run my fingers across the sofa, chewing on my inner cheek as I look around the room. A picture of a dog sits on her desk, with big brown eyes. I stare at it for at least five minutes before I find words. "I have a lot of baggage." I don't take my eyes off the picture. "And I'm worried nobody can fix me."

"What makes you think that?"

I finally look at her, fixating on her left shoulder as I respond, "Well, I was raised by a woman who hated me, a dad who skipped town the minute I was walking, and don't get me started on all of my mom's ex's." *Or mine.*

"Okay, is there a topic you want to unpack first?"

I look at her, words unexpectedly tumbling out of my mouth. "How can you erase twenty-four years of someone breaking you apart piece by piece? How do I learn to love myself when all she ever taught me was how to hate myself?"

Dr. Boate doesn't skip a beat, leaning forward in her chair, a flicker of sadness filling her eyes. "It'll take some time, and it won't be easy, but we'll get there."

I stare back at the dog in the photo, praying that there is truth to her words.

And that, little by little, I can heal all the scars I've physically and emotionally received over the years.

Chapter 7

WYATT

Scott and Ellie have been a power couple for all of four months and they've already organized a community event with face painting, baked goods, barbecued food, a petting zoo, and more. All money raised will be going towards Habitat for Humanity.

I seriously don't know when either of them sleeps.

I'm half convinced that if they'd started dating years ago that they would have found a way to solve world hunger or something.

They even splurged on getting us T-shirts that say, "Elm Woods Crew."

Ellie approaches me with a familiar face beside her.

Whitney.

She has the same light green shirt that I do, but hers looks much cuter and man does it make her eyes shine.

"Morning, Ellie. Morning, Whitney," I greet them, tilting my head in a slight nod.

"Hey," Ellie answers, getting right to business, as usual. "I have to run to the office; can you help Whitney with the face painting? Paige had a last-minute interior design consultation, so she won't be here until later this afternoon."

Part of me wants to tell Ellie that I can't draw to save my life, but a breeze causes me to catch a whiff of Whitney's shampoo. She smells like fresh flowers.

No harm in keeping her company.

"Sure," I reply.

"Great. Cool. Okay." Ellie claps her hands together. "Well, have fun." She looks between Whitney and I, except the look she gives Whitney is one of reassurance and the one she gives me screams, "Don't break my friend or I'll hurt you."

Whitney walks beside me to the booth in an awkward silence. I get the vibe that I wasn't her first choice, but that doesn't mean I can't make the most of our time together.

"Have you painted peoples' faces before?" I ask, and then smack my hand against my forehead as I take in her eyeshadow and mascara. "I mean, never mind . . . you're wearing makeup—it's sort of the same thing."

She raises an eyebrow at me, so I let out a strained laugh. "No? They're different things, huh? Sorry."

After a long pause she finally says, "I've done makeup for many people in my life, but I've never turned them into a butterfly."

My mouth twitches. "Fair enough. Well, I guess it's a first for both of us."

She moves diligently, preparing paint brushes and the containers of paint into a straight line as the first group of children approach us.

"Good morning." Her face breaks into a wide grin as she takes in a little girl wearing a tiger costume.

"Hi. I'm Mimi, I like turtles, do you?" the girl asks, sitting on one of the chairs.

"I love turtles! Any animals, really . . . tigers are super cool too," Whitney says with an enthusiastic nod, motioning towards the girl's outfit.

I barely notice a little boy sitting in front of me, because I'm so entranced with how engaging she is with the girl—how attentive she is.

We spend the next hour painting all sorts of things–flowers, spiders, sports logos, zombie faces, and the entire time, she is lit up like a Christmas tree, beaming and laughing with each child she worked on. It's the most beautiful sound I've heard in my life.

When there is finally a lull in people coming by, I turn to face her. "You're much better at face painting than I am."

She lets out a small laugh. "barely."

I readjust my hat. "I'm pretty sure I saw a mother wipe her kids face paint off. My pumpkin looked more like a rotting orange."

Her lip twitches. "*Oh.* That . . . was a pumpkin?"

I cross my arms, unable to contain my laughter at her sudden sass. "Ouch. Break my heart, why don't you?"

"Sorry." Her shoulders sink a bit.

"Hey, I was joking." I keep my tone soft. Her eyes find mine again, and something causes me to say, "Besides, if anyone's heart was broken, it was probably that poor kid. Good thing they aren't paying us!"

"Oh, no. No way, don't lump me in with you. I've pulled my weight very well, thank you very much. You'd be fired, not me."

Before I can make a comeback, two girls come running towards Whitney full speed. "Auntie Whitney!" they call out, hugging her. "We missed you so much."

Grant and Bree follow behind, wrapped up in each other.

"Hi, girls! You both look beautiful today, are you wearing new hair bows?" She touches the bows in their hair.

"Yes! Mommy bought them for us!" one of them says, before eyeing me. "Are you Auntie Whitney's boyfriend?"

"Chloe," Bree says with a firm mom voice. "We don't ask people personal questions, especially in public."

Grant and Bree give Whitney a hug before hugging me as well.

Chloe is bouncing on her heels when she asks, "Can I at least learn his name?"

I chuckle, crouching to her level. "My name is Wyatt."

"Wyatt. Hm." She turns to Grant and says, "Work Wyatt?"

I give Grant a smirk. "Talking about me at home, Thompson?"

He chuckles and whispers something to his daughters, who proceed to squeal before turning towards me. Chloe exclaims, "Daddy said you want us to paint *your* face."

I give him a side eye, before turning towards his daughters with a smile. "I'd love that! Thank you, girls."

Five minutes and a very wet, uncomfortable face later, Grant is taking my picture and a group of people have gathered around us.

I face Whitney, appreciating her attempt to not laugh. "How do I look?"

"You're the prettiest butterfly I've ever seen." Her lips press together tightly, but the subtle shaking of her body gives her away.

"I feel like it will be a pain to wash out of my stubble." I pull my phone out, looking at my reflection on the screen. "And they used up the entire jar of purple paint."

"I don't blame them; purple is my favorite." Whitney is quiet as she says it, straightening out the brushes she just washed off. "Also just use warm water and soap, it should all come out after one or two tries.

You might not want to shave for a day or two, in case it irritates your sk–sorry . . ." She trails off.

I give her a confused look. "Why are you sorry? That was great advice. I kind of assumed I should use some sort of cream or body wash for it."

"Oh, just . . . you didn't ask for my advice." She fidgets with her fingers, looking away from me. "I didn't mean to overstep."

How she says it unlocks a memory I haven't thought about in years.

My dad throws his glass across the room, the glass shattering beside Wesley's highchair. I stare down at the mashed potatoes on my plate, knowing that me speaking up would only make things worse.

"Robert, please." My mom's voice is shaky. "I didn't mean to overstep or upset you. I just don't want the boys seeing you like this."

"I don't need to talk to a therapist, that's for weak people. I am not a weak man. Who fucking cares if I have a drink with dinner. The boys are too young and dumb to notice. They'll be fine." His chair scrapes against the floor. "And clean up this mess. I don't need my boys thinking they can leave their shit everywhere."

Once the front door slams, I finally let myself look up.

My mother's sobs are silent as she holds her head in her hands. She's mastered the art of crying quietly. As she cries, I clean up the glass, whispering the words she stopped saying a long time ago. "Things will get better. Tomorrow is a new day."

I don't think either of us believe that's true.

But at eleven, there isn't much more I can do.

Chapter 8

WHITNEY

When Paige shows up to relieve Wyatt, part of me is disappointed to watch him leave. Unlike most other men, I feel a sense of calm around him, and Paige is staring at me as if she can tell.

"Do you want to go grab some food?" she asks me, nudging my shoulder. "I assume you didn't eat yet?" My stomach grumbles in response so she pulls me out of the chair I'm sitting in. "Go ahead. Grant is at the food stand with Scott," Paige tells me.

"Thanks. I'll be back in a bit."

"No rush, Whit."

I move through the crowd, locking onto Grant's familiar figure. It's something my therapist suggested—keeping my eye on a safe space in an unfamiliar place. But as I move closer towards the food stand, another pair of eyes locks on mine. The caramel-colored ones I just spent the better part of four hours trying not to stare at.

"Did you get fired too?" Wyatt teases when I reach them.

I shake my head. "No, Paige told me I should eat something."

I pick up a plastic plate and Grant starts to pile some stuff on it for me, while I scope out the picnic benches.

"Here ya go." Grant hands me my plate back and I mumble out a *thanks* before grabbing a water bottle and moving towards the furthest bench.

A moment later Wyatt sits down across from me.

"You cool if I sit here? Or are you sick of me and my butterfly-filled face?" He motions to his overly purple face.

I chew my lip, trying to keep my laugh in. "You can stay," I offer.

He gives me a gentle smile and says, "Thank you," before taking a bite of his burger.

"So, what do you do for work, Whitney? Or are you in school?" he asks me casually but it's enough to make me stare at my hands. "Or . . . sorry, that's personal, you don't need to answer."

"No, it's, uh . . . okay. I'm between jobs right now. Ellie is trying to convince me to take a job with her, which is part of why she dragged me here today."

Wyatt smiles thoughtfully before saying, "I mean, we always need another person to put up cupboards and nail shingles into the roof."

I stare down at my flowy dress and laugh. "I've actually never used a hammer before."

He lets out a chuckle. "Well, you're never too old to learn!"

I find myself rolling my eyes, something I usually save for people I trust, so it catches me off guard how comfortable I seem to feel around him. "No, she wants me to be her office administrator."

His eyes widen, as if he's impressed. "That's awesome. You're going to take it I assume?"

"I don't . . . I'm . . . it's complicated." I refuse to meet his eyes as I speak.

His tone is soft as he says, "If it's fear holding you back, you should say 'fuck it.' If it's something you want to do and are good at, why not give yourself the chance to find out?"

I try not to laugh at the fact my therapist had told me something similar yesterday–without the "fuck it" part.

"I was nervous about working for Scott, of letting him down because I was fresh out of high school, but he took me under his wing without blinking, and if I've learned anything over the last few months, it's that Ellie and Scott are very similar. And they always want what's best for their business and friends."

I finally allow myself to look at Wyatt and I regret it instantly. He's wearing a sheepish grin and his eyes are sparkling as the sun shifts behind a cloud.

Even with a lopsided butterfly, he's handsome.

My eyes trail to where Ellie and Scott are standing, smiling and greeting everyone coming and going. He's right. Ellie is right. I deserve this and I should do this.

I will do this.

I take a sip of my water and shift the conversation towards safe subjects. Face painting, houses, Ellie and Scott.

I eat slowly and I'd like to think he's matching my pace because he also doesn't want this moment to slip away.

As we clean up our plates, Wyatt clears his throat and a nervous expression crosses his face before he says, "So, I was wondering if I could grab your number."

"Uh . . . sure," I reply as he pulls his phone out of his pocket, handing it to me.

I type in my information and when I hand it back, he smiles. "Whitney Harris. I like it." His hand reaches towards mine and I realize he wants to shake my hand. "Morgan; Wyatt Morgan.

"Good detective name," I reply with a laugh, as I stand with my plate and move towards the garbage can.

He follows beside me. "Whitney Harris sounds fancy, like you could be attending high tea with world leaders."

I snort, covering my mouth. "I can guarantee I'll never be having fancy parties with world leaders. I was named after my dad's ex-girlfriend."

Why the heck did I just say that?

Wyatt frowns. "Your mom didn't know, I assume?"

"Not until after the papers were signed." I shrug. Maybe that was what started her hatred for me. That, and the fact I'm the spitting image of my dad, allegedly—he didn't stick around long enough for me to know.

Don't get in your head right now . . .

"Wow, that's not cool. Your poor mom." His voice pulls me back to reality, like a little nudge.

If only he knew.

I look down at the ground and kick a pebble.

"You okay . . .?"

I look up at him, giving a small nod. "Yeah . . . just zoned out a bit."

His expression falters, meaning he knows I'm lying, but I doubt he'll try and pry.

"I've had fun with you today, Whitney Harris." The statement catches me off guard and a flutter of butterflies erupts in my stomach.

I wonder if they're purple like the one on his face.

"Me too," I reply honestly. "Anyway, I should probably get back to Paige now."

"Yeah, no worries. I'll see you later." He gives me an awkward wave before backing away from me slowly, his eyes locked on mine, until I finally will myself to look away.

When I reach Paige, she looks at the invisible watch on her wrist. "Excuse me? Where have you been hiding?"

"I was eating with Wyatt." I try to sound nonchalant, but the fact that my cheeks hurt from smiling for the first time in weeks is all the proof anyone needs to know that I'm feeling at peace.

"Oh, were you now?" Her eyebrows wiggle up and down.

"Don't start." I shove her shoulder with a laugh. She eyes me, expecting me to elaborate but I just offer her a shrug. "He's just easy to talk to."

Paige leans back in her chair. "I know, Whit. Just seeing you walk around with a smile on your face is a nice change."

After the event, I help drop a few supplies off at Ellie's offices and as she checks her email, the words slip out, "I want to work for you."

"Say it again." Ellie's body is vibrating as I stand in her office doorway.

I groan, leaning against the door frame. "Elenor Elm, can I pretty please take a job as your office administrator?"

She jumps up and down, before consuming me in a tight hug. "Heck yes lady! Come on then, we have a million things to sort out and prepare for. This is the most exciting day of my life."

I shake my head. "Shouldn't it be the best day of *my* life?"

"Technically, but I've already asked so much of you, I don't want to push things by assuming that it actually is. I feel like your best day includes pancakes, horses, and grilled cheese sandwiches for dinner." She gives me a knowing smile.

The Scout Special.

"Don't forget the extra pickles." I laugh as she leads me down the hallway to an office.

"Okay, this will be your office, but don't get too comfortable here. We might be looking for a new building sooner than later. Also, that is top secret so shh, don't tell anyone."

I give her a look as if to say, "Who would I tell?" and she lets out a long laugh.

"This will be so fun. Let me find the contract for you to review. You hang out here, figure out if you find the chair comfortable," Ellie says quickly before heading back down the hallway.

Sitting down at the desk, I let out a contented sigh. Today I've felt a sense of purpose I haven't had in years. I'm glad that Ellie brought me to the fundraiser and I'm glad that someone other than my therapist told me to say, "fuck it."

Maybe I'm getting the hang of this whole healing thing.

A sharp voice sounds in my head. *Really? You thought it would be that easy?*

Maybe not . . .

Chapter 9

WYATT

*W*hitney Harris. The way she looked over her shoulder at me once she reached the face painting booth, with twinkling eyes, tells me that I'm a goner.

Her long blonde hair and green doe eyes had everyone checking her out, but it was *me* she was talking to, *me* she was laughing with.

I can sense her walls are high and she doesn't soften to strangers easily, so knowing I'm breaking through the cracks slightly gives me a sense of pride I never imagined having.

She was right about it taking two, very thorough, face washes to get the purple off my face.

I draft about fifteen texts to her before finally hitting send.

Wyatt: Hey Whitney, thanks for being the best face painting partner. We might need to go into business someday.

Whitney: No offense, Wyatt but I think we'd go bankrupt very quickly.

Her response makes me chuckle, especially when I see the pumpkin emoji.

Wyatt: True, but the company would be great.

Whitney: Speak for yourself

Wyatt: Ouch.

Whitney: Also I said fuck it.

It takes my brain a moment to realize she means she took the job with Ellie.

Wyatt: Congrats! This is a huge deal.

Whitney: If it's any consolation, you kind of helped motivate me to do it. I'm honestly not sure I would have taken it if I didn't work up the courage to do it today.

A sense of pride fills my heart at her taking a step in the right direction, especially knowing that I played even a small role in her being brave enough to do it.

We text back and forth for the rest of the evening and by the time I get into bed my face hurts from smiling.

Is tomorrow too soon to ask her on a date?

I feel my phone buzz in my pocket as we're loading up the trucks at the end of my workday and I can't help but smile.

Whitney: Happy Wednesday, Wyatt! Hope you had a good day at work!

"Who is making you smile, Wyatt?" Ellie leans against my truck suddenly, making me jump.

"Nobody," I reply quickly.

"Mhmm, you're a terrible liar, Wyatt Morgan." She laughs before adding, "I'm not completely oblivious to the fact you and one of my best friends have been texting back and forth for a week . . ."

"There's no secrets in this world, are there?" I joke as her brown eyes land on mine.

"Are you going to take her on a date?" She's bouncing around me like an overly excited dog.

"Good Lord, Ellie. Did you have extra coffee today?" I chuckle, putting my hands on her shoulders. "Relax, I'm working up to it," I promise.

She holds up her hands in defense. "Sorry, sorry. I'm an over-eager friend."

"You're telling me."

Worry crosses her face and her eyebrows come together. "Wyatt, she's been through a lot . . . and I just want what's best for her. Go easy on her, please."

I squeeze her shoulder, giving her a pointed look. "I will, Ellie. But you gotta go easy on me too, I won't rush her into something she's not ready for."

Ellie gives a small nod, worry still covering her face.

"Seriously, Ellie, I don't plan to hurt her. I'm guessing she's had enough of that in life."

Her eyes widen as realization hits her that I know at least a little about Whitney's past. I hope she doesn't get mad at Scott for telling me.

I shift so I can open my truck door. "She and I have a lot more in common than you know. I'll see you tomorrow."

Ellie backs up slowly, and her eyebrows furrow as if she's trying to connect the dots.

As soon as I get in my truck, I dial my mom's number—I call her every Wednesday. After my dad died, my mom and younger brother moved to Springfield to get a fresh start and get away from the bad memories our house carried. She wanted me to come too, but by that point I was already renting my apartment and working as Scott's right-hand man.

She answers immediately. "Hi, Wyatt. How was work today?"

I dive into telling her about our new project and then I tell her about my week and the fundraiser. I ramble on, not letting her get a word in.

"Wyatt . . . circle back for a second. Who is Whitney?" my mom basically shouts over me.

"Oh." I chuckle. "She's one of Ellie's best friends."

"Hm, is she pretty?" my mom asks with excitement in her voice.

"Breathtaking, Mom." I sigh.

"Is that so? Are you going to ask her out?" I imagine her jumping up and down excitedly, much like Ellie.

"Quite possibly." I laugh, stopping at a stop sign.

"I'm beaming over here, Wyatt." She laughs out. "Can't remember the last time you talked to me about a girl! Hang on, Wesley just got home."

I smile as my brother calls out, "Hi, loser."

"Hi, nerd. How was band practice today?"

"Spectacular. I'm working on my drum solo."

It's funny how much the family dynamics change when the monsters don't haunt us every single day.

Chapter 10

WHITNEY

Wyatt and I are hanging out today. I can't remember the last time I've hung out with a guy one-on-one, as friends. I'm freaking out as I walk down main street, trying to calm my jittery hands. When he texted me last night asking me to meet him at Parnassus Books, I felt giddy. Books are my escape from reality—a safe haven.

Growing up I spent a lot of time hiding at the library and bookstores, trying to make sense of addiction and how to cope with pain and isolation. But the library and bookstores became a second home to me. If April and Scout weren't available to care for me, I would alternate between bookstores and craft stores.

Escaping into fairytales and sewing made everything hurt less.

Temporarily at least.

I stand outside the bookstore, looking in the window, trying to fight down my anxiety.

What if everything so far has just been an act and he'll show his true colors once I let my guard down?

We've been texting throughout the week, and he's been so nice and attentive, especially when I told him I worked up the courage to tell Ellie I'd take the job. He even texted me on my first day to wish me luck. Ellie has me doing training and refreshment courses this week, and next week I'll have to read through the policies and company standards–something that excites me far more than most normal people.

"Whitney!" I turn towards the voice and my heart begins to race. Wyatt is standing beside me, wearing a striped, blue T-shirt with black jeans and has his Woods Construction hat on backwards.

"Jesus, you look gorgeous today," he tells me once he reaches me.

"Hey." I give him a small smile, consumed by nerves. *He's really got to stop wearing his hat backwards or I'm going to have a hard time just being friends with him.*

"Shall we?" He tilts his head towards the store and then holds the door open for me. I falter and I see confusion cross his face.

"I'm not exactly used to men being chivalrous," I say quietly as I pass him. The subtle scent of his body fills my nose, something outdoorsy.

"I wouldn't say holding the door open is chivalrous. I think you've been hanging out with the wrong kind of men," he jokes.

He has no idea.

I self-consciously lead us towards the romance section and Wyatt follows behind me without complaint as I slowly scan the row.

"What kind of books do you like to read most?" he asks me as I pull a book off the shelf and read the synopsis on the back.

I squint my eyes and laugh. "I love books that make me cry, and books that make my heart explode into a million pieces. What kind of books do you like?" I reply as I continue to scan the bookshelf.

"I like the classics, *To Kill a Mockingbird*, *Animal Farm* . . . anything that was published before we ever existed in this world. I like reading fiction from the past."

I didn't expect that response. My shock isn't hard to see.

"Ah, you don't like the classics?"

"No, I do. *To Kill a Mockingbird* is one of my favorite books," I respond, shaking my head.

"Are you just saying that?"

"No, my best friend's grandma used to read it to us all the time, her name was Jean Louise so April and I would call her Scout as a joke, but it stuck." I look down at my feet with a sad smile.

Wyatt's lip twitches. "April is the girl who came with you to Scott's birthday, yeah?"

I nod, exhaling. "Yeah."

His finger grazes the side of my pinky. "So Grandma Scout, did she read you any other good books?"

The question is so simple, so casual but it makes me look up. "The entire Nancy Drew collection, most of Shakespeare's plays, Narnia, Lord of the Rings . . . way too many. One summer she read us a bunch of books with a bunch of butterfly facts and now they're ingrained in my head."

"Wow, you must have spent a lot of time together, huh?" Something shifts in his voice, as if he's trying to piece together my childhood.

I focus on the shelf ahead of me. "Her farm was my favorite place."

"So, tell me a fun fact about butterflies then, besides the fact that I look super as one," he says with a smirk.

"There are over 24,000 species of butterflies and they cannot fly if their body temperature is less than eighty-six degrees," I throw out casually.

Wyatt pulls out his phone. "That was oddly specific. I have to fact check." He types on his phone and lets out a whistle. "Color me impressed, what strange facts to know. If there's ever a butterfly trivia night in town, I know who to call!"

I let out a snort, covering my mouth. "Oh hush."

Stop snorting, dammit.

Wyatt clears his throat and picks a book off the shelf. "What about this one? It has a fun cover."

I try not to laugh at Wyatt picking out one of my latest favorite books. "Are you telling me you judge a book by its cover, Wyatt?" I tease.

He chuckles, putting it back on the shelf before smiling at me. "No, truthfully I prefer to read the books with boring covers because oftentimes going into the story blind makes for an interesting reading experience."

I don't know what I expected out of him, but this wasn't it.

We walk through every aisle and Wyatt picks random books up for us to admire as we discuss which TV shows and movies were a letdown after reading the books.

"What about *The Hunger Games*?" he asks.

I groan, pursing my lips. "That one is tough, I can never tell if I loved the movies because they were good, or because I thought Peeta and Gale were hot."

Wyatt snorts. "When was the last time you watched it?"

I chew my lip, trying to remember. "It's been a long time."

"Well, a refresh might benefit you then."

Is he suggesting we watch it together?

"Did you read the series?" I ask him.

"Yes . . . And I liked the movies, but now I'm wondering if Jennifer Lawrence is the only reason. Maybe we're both just shallow!"

We chuckle, staring at each other for a moment before I look away and move down another row.

Once we finish scanning the entire store, Wyatt eyes me excitedly. "I want you to pick one book and I'm going to buy it for you," he tells me.

"Oh no, you don't have to do that," I protest, shaking my head.

"I want to. Either you decide on one, or I can probably recount at least four books you stood in front of for too long and I'll buy you all of them. Consider it a gift to celebrate your new job," he challenges.

I would never let him buy me four books, and I'm pretty sure he's figured that out.

Moving towards one of the rows, I grab *Animal Farm* off the shelf.

Might as well try something new and since it's one of his favorite books, it might be nice to see inside his mind.

"Have you ever read it before?" he asks, and I shake my head. He smiles as I hand him the book. "You're either going to love it or hate it. No one ever really falls in the middle."

Chapter 11

WYATT

"Thanks for the book," Whitney repeats for the sixth time as we walk into the coffee shop. The smell of fresh baked croissants fills the air and I see Whitney eye the pastries with happiness.

"Stop thanking me, you might hate it." I step beside her, trying and failing for the hundredth time to not check her out. She's wearing a long dress covered in flowers and a jean jacket with her long blonde hair left down.

"Good afternoon, what can I get you folks?" The cashier says when we approach the counter.

Whitney looks up at me and her expression is uncertain. *Does she expect me to order for her? Or is she unsure if she's allowed to get something?*

"I'll have a black coffee and a blueberry muffin," I say before eyeing Whitney. "What would you like?"

She looks caught off guard and hesitates to answer. "I'll have a small peach tea, please," she says quietly.

I let my finger graze her thumb, seeing if it'll make her a bit less guarded.

She shimmies her shoulders back and I assume she's giving herself an internal pep talk. "Sorry. I'll have a medium peach tea and a butter croissant, please," she tells the cashier before looking at me as I pay. "Is that okay?"

"Whitney, you can have whatever you want, alright? You don't need my permission for anything," I tell her as we move to the end of the counter to wait for our orders. "Do you want to sit inside or outside?" I ask her.

Again, she looks shocked that I'm asking for her input. She looks between the patio and indoor seating. "Outside please . . . unless you'd rather sit inside." She looks flustered.

"Outside works for me," I say, trying to reassure her.

"Here you go!" one of the workers calls out, placing our stuff on the ledge.

"Thank you," Whitney and I both say in unison, before grabbing our drinks and food.

We sit down at a table, and she looks at me as if she wants to say something, but instead Whitney looks out to the street.

I sip my coffee, watching her. I'm coming to realize she spends a lot of time chewing on the inside of her cheek. I can't figure out if it's a nervous tick, or a calming habit.

Her hair moves in the breeze as her eyes find mine again.

"What's on your mind?" I ask her, hoping she doesn't think I'm creepy for watching her.

She opens her mouth once, chews the inside of her cheek, opens her mouth again and repeats the action at least five more times. "Are you just hanging out with me because our best friends are dating . . . or did Ellie tell you to spend time with me, or . . . ?"

She doesn't look straight at me as she asks and I exhale, clenching my jaw. "No, Whitney, you're good company. I'm here with you because I want to be here with you. And at the end of the date, I'm going to ask you on another date because I—as a grown man—want to. Okay?"

She swallows and her cheeks go red. "O-oh . . . this is a date? Okay." She takes a sip of her tea and I don't miss how her cup shakes as she brings it to her lips.

Shit. I never said it was a date, did I? No. I just asked her to hang out. Idiot.

"Do you want this to be a date?" I raise an eyebrow at her and her lips twitch.

"Um . . . I guess so." Her shoulders relax and she takes a bite of her croissant.

I steer the conversation back to safe topics, asking her how many books she reads and what else she does for fun, and it leads to her telling me about how she sews. She tells me that she and April try to go to a sewing workshop once a month and that she's even sewn some of her own clothes.

"My mom tried once . . . she never really got the knack for it," I tell her.

Whitney gives me a nod. "Oh, yeah . . . you need a whole lot of patience when you're first starting out. But now it's second nature to me."

"That's so cool, I'm not crafty at all . . . I don't have the patience for that sort of thing."

"It took a long time for me to get the hang of it, my tension was always way too loose, but now I could probably do it with my eyes shut."

"Gah, I'd be too worried about sewing the fabric to my hand."

Whitney takes a sip of her drink before saying, "Been there, done that. I don't recommend it."

Everything I learn about her makes me want to stay and talk to her all evening, but I have a guy's night to go to tonight, and I'm not sure I want to bring her to meet my friends after one date. Not that I don't think they'd enjoy her, I just have a sense that Whitney would run at the first sign of commitment or pressure.

We walk down the main drag of Nashville for a bit before she turns to me and says, "I should probably head home." She fidgets with her jacket. "Thanks for a great day, Wyatt. I look forward to starting the book." She motions to her bag containing *Animal Farm*.

"Maybe once you finish the book we can move on to the biggest question in life," I say. She tilts her head up at me with confusion, so I lean towards her. "If we're just shallow, or if *The Hunger Games* is an actual cinematic masterpiece."

She lets out a long laugh, before biting her lip. "Oh gosh, I forgot about Finnick!"

"Who?"

"Finnick. You know, tall, dirty blond hair . . . his death makes me sob like an idiot," she says matter-of-factly.

"Ah, you're into tall blondes, are you?" I tease.

She doesn't miss a beat, leaning up to kiss my cheek. "I might be. See ya later, Wyatt."

I watch as she walks down the street with a false sense of confidence. I can't help but assume it took her every ounce of courage to kiss me.

And I'm disappointed with myself that she beat me to it.

I head to my friend Mark's house where my other childhood friends are also waiting for me.

"You're late, Wyatt. You're never late," Frankie calls out. Austin and Mark are nodding along with him.

"Yeah, well there's a first time for everything." I hug Mark before dropping down to the table, placing the case of beer beside me.

The three of them stare at me, waiting for further explanation but I just shrug.

"At least he brought beer!" Mark chimes in.

"So where were you, hmm?" Austin leans towards me. The three of them are still staring.

"I was on a date," I say, pulling a beer out for each of us.

"A what?" Frankie almost drops his can.

"Don't make a big deal of it, Jesus." I roll my eyes, grabbing poker chips from the middle of the table.

"Hmm," comes from all three of them.

"Knock, knock," sounds from the front door as Scott and Grant enter. "Sorry we're late, I got roped into playing barbies with two lovely ladies." Scott chuckles as he and Grant sit down.

"Don't worry, Wyatt just got here too. He was late."

Scott smirks at me and opens his mouth to speak.

I shoot him daggers. "Don't."

"Seriously, you told Scott before telling us?" Mark pretends to stab himself in the heart. "Does twenty-two years of friendship mean nothing anymore?"

"I mean . . . she *is* one of Ellie's best friends," Grant adds casually, taking a sip of his beer.

Such a traitor.

"Grant too?" Austin groans. "What happened to loyalty?"

Frankie turns to Scott. "Since he's being so secretive, I'll ask you. Is it Paige from the show?"

"Nope." He beams, as if him knowing something they don't is the greatest accomplishment of his life.

"She's new to the company, but she's been in Ellie's life for years," Grant adds.

"Guys!" I huff out.

Scott pulls out his phone and I see him open Instagram. I know which picture he's pulling up—it's the one that led me to creep on Whitney's profile a few nights ago. It's a picture of Ellie, Whitney, Paige, Bree, and April from last Sunday. They're all covered with flour, surrounded by fresh baked cookies on the counter, beaming.

"The blonde on the left," Scott says. "Whitney."

"Damn, Wyatt. Look at her!" Frankie exclaims, pointing the phone towards me.

Even though I've stared at it far too many times already, I can't help but smile.

"What a bunch of beauties." Austin whistles out. "Which of them is single?"

"For you? None of them," Grant chimes in, making us all laugh.

"Well, did you hold hands? Did you kiss her? Tell us everything." Mark flutters his eyelashes, leaning onto his hand like some love-sick puppy.

I glare at him. "You guys are making me regret being here."

Frankie pats my back. "We're just giving you a hard time. If it helps, just remember it took Scott seven years to get a girlfriend."

Scott swats his head. "Hey, now. But seriously, how was your date? Don't skimp on details or I'll get the Ellie version and you know she won't leave out a single thing Whitney tells her."

Mark starts shuffling cards. "And then he'll call us and fill us in, like a *good* friend."

"I bought her *Animal Farm*."

The looks around the table are priceless.

"Welp, looks like you'll end up dumped before you even get together, seems like I'll have a chance after all," Austin teases.

Maybe I should have bought her another book instead.

Chapter 12

WHITNEY

I t's taking some time adjusting to working an 8-4 work day, but it's at least helping regulate my sleep again. Instead of being up half the night, I'm now falling asleep before eleven.

Ellie has, unsurprisingly, been the best boss and has slowly been introducing me to the staff. Day by day I'm personalizing my office space with pictures and some plants.

Now the next step is to find an apartment that I can actually afford. Everything affordable is a few streets too close for comfort to my mom's house–I'd rather not take a step backwards.

April and Kyle are sitting watching TV when I get home from work.

I give them a small nod before moving to the spare bedroom, switching into sweatpants. Grabbing the book Wyatt bought me, I move into the living room, settling on the love seat.

"How was work?" April asks me.

"Good. I should have enough saved up for a place again in no time," I say, looking down.

"Hey. Stop that." April sighs quietly. "This is your home for as long as you need, Whit."

I give her a sad smile and open my book. Every time I bring it up she reassures me, but I still worry that I'm bothering them. And honestly, I want to know what it feels like to have a place of my own.

My eyes scan the page before me, and I quickly feel my eyes criss-cross.

Animal Farm is boring. I can usually binge read a book in a few hours but as I sit on the couch beside April and Kyle, trying to get into the book for the fourth time this week, I groan and throw the book down. "Why does he enjoy this book?"

Kyle laughs. "Maybe he likes Russian history."

I stare at him in confusion.

"It's basically about the events of Russia's Bolshevik revolution and the betrayal of the cause by Joseph Stalin.", he says casually, as if everyone would know that fact.

It is?

April snorts, shaking her head. "How do you even know that? Do you like the book, Kyle?" April raises an eyebrow. In the six years I've known Kyle, I've never seen him read a single book.

"It's not bad. I was able to bullshit my way through an essay for it in high school. So, it's one of those facts that stays with me—like a catchy commercial jingle. Not one I would read every day," he says nonchalantly. "Maybe the hottie is also a smartie pants? He likes books that make you think?"

"Okay, please never say hottie about anyone but me . . . ever." April snorts again, before turning to face me. "You should call him and complain about how boring it is . . . make him take you out on another date or something. It is Friday night after all, you got to live a little."

I roll my eyes. "I'm not going to call him, that seems forward. But I get it. You two want alone time. I'm sorry." I stand quickly.

April sits up, grabbing my hand. "That's not what I meant . . . We just don't want you feeling like we have you on a curfew, or that you have to sit through *Married at First Sight* reruns with us. You aren't trapped in the house." Her eyes find mine. "This isn't a prison cell or a punishment."

We have a silent discussion with our eyes before she stands and pulls me into a hug. "You could live with us forever if you needed to, Scout's honor. I love you, Whit."

"Yeah, we love you Whitney, our house is your house. If anything, April will kick me out before she kicks you out," Kyle jokes, making us all laugh.

"Thanks . . . for . . . well, you know. Everything," I say, blinking back tears.

April hugs me again before I head back into their guest bedroom.

It's barely 7:30 PM, I could go out and do something. I could call Wyatt. But what if he's busy? What if he thinks I'm lame for reading on a Friday night.

I stare down at my phone for five minutes before I text him.

Whitney: I regret you buying me *Animal Farm*.

Bubbles appear on the screen once, twice, three times. But nothing comes through.

He's busy.

My spine tingles as my mom's voice whispers, *"Nobody has time for a waste like you."*

But when my phone rings, and his name shows up on the screen, I squeal.

"Uh, hi," I answer, after letting it ring four times.

"Are you reading *Animal Farm* on a Friday night?" He sounds amused.

"I . . . wouldn't call it reading . . . dragging my feet maybe, or pulling my eyes out of their sockets."

His laughter is loud and contagious.

"Whitney Harris, you poor thing. I might need to rescue you before you pull those beautiful green eyes out of your beautiful face."

I bite my lip, blushing.

That was two beautiful's in one sentence.

"I don't know, Wyatt . . . I'm already on my way to the torture chamber to put myself out of my misery," I say with an even voice.

He laughs again. "Nope. Not happening. I will not have this. I volunteer as tribute."

I giggle.

"But seriously, I'm around to occupy your time . . . Oh, god that came out wrong. I, uh . . ."

I walk towards my closet and pull out an outfit, suddenly feeling the urge to go to one of my favorite places, and for some reason, I want him to come with me. "Want to meet me somewhere?"

"As long as it's not a torture chamber, yes," he says eagerly, and I hear the smile in his voice.

"Okay. I'll text you the address and meet you there at 8:30 PM," I offer, slipping out of my sweatpants.

"Mysterious. I like it."

"See ya in a bit, Wyatt."

When I walked out into the living room with my riding boots and hair braided back, April didn't hesitate to drive me, even though I told her I could take an uber.

I stand in front of the building waiting for him to arrive. I should have told him what to wear. Hopefully he's not dressed for a fancy dinner.

When I see a black pick-up truck pull up, goosebumps cover my arms.

And then, when he hops out of the truck wearing blue jeans and a plaid button up my mouth goes dry. His hair is tousled to perfection.

"Feels like I'm about to be murdered," he teases as he approaches me. When he leans forward to hug me, I'm consumed by his scent. I can never fully pinpoint what he smells like, but it smells fresh and calming. "You look beautiful, Whitney," he whispers against my forehead, his mouth grazing my skin.

"I won't murder you, don't worry." I laugh, pulling away from him hesitantly.

The front door opens, making Wyatt jump.

I smirk up at him.

"Ready, Whitney?"

I turn towards Crystal with excitement. "Yup! This is Wyatt," I reply, moving forward, letting my cowgirl boots crunch on the gravel.

She gives him a wave and he offers her a nod in return. "Nice to meet you."

Wyatt falls in step beside me as we move through the barn. When we get to the horse stables Crystal gives me a final hug. "Just come to the main house, or text me when you finish up here. John and I can clean up."

"Thanks, Crystal," I reply.

"Ronald is in the last stall," she calls over her shoulder.

I step further into the stables, the sound of neighing filling the space. I move to the last stall excitedly, and there she is, in all her glory . . . yes, *she*.

Ronald's mom belonged to Scout, so after she died, and the horses were distributed, April and I were still able to visit and keep in touch. Most of them came to Crystal's farm. Ronald was my favorite horse, probably because she kept me sane through some of the worst years of my life. We named her Ronald as a joke, but now she's one of the best show horses around.

"Hey, girl," I say as I approach her. She comes over to me and I rub her silky mane. "You look gorgeous today." She snorts at me, and I laugh, leaning against her, feeling instantly calm. If I had my way I'd be surrounded by horses every day of my life. They've always been therapeutic to me.

They always remind me of Scout.

"I wouldn't have pegged you for a horse girl," Wyatt says thoughtfully, leaning against the gate alongside me. He sticks his hand towards Ronald, and she moves towards him. He scratches the side of her face and I feel my mouth hang open as I watch him, looking rugged and sexy, being so gentle.

"I love horses," I say quietly. "Especially Ronald."

"You'll have to fill me in on how she got her name." His eyes lock with mine, making my heart skip a beat.

"I will." I give him a small smile before turning back to Ronald, giving her one last pat. "Do you know how to ride?"

Wyatt smiles down at me. "Sure do. You tell me which horse is mine for the night and I'll saddle them up."

Jesus, where has this man been all my life?

"You can have Jinxie or Jeff."

I point to the two horses in the stalls to our left and he takes them both in. Jeff is dark, almost black—similar to Ronald—whereas Jinxie is a light gray.

"Is Jeff also a girl?" he asks with a chuckle. And as I nod, his laughter only gets louder. "God, you're too much, you know that right?"

"No idea what you're talking about!" I feign innocence as I enter Ronald's stall.

"Hiya, Jeff," he calls out as he moves towards her.

We saddle up the horses in silence—crystal had done most of the prep work for us before we got here. When the horses are both ready, I motion for Wyatt to follow me to the arena.

"Wow, this is incredible." He whistles, looking around the large space.

Once we get into the ring, Ronald and Jeff stand perfectly still, waiting for us to mount them.

"Look at you two showing off," Wyatt teases, rubbing Jeff's mane. "Do you need help up Whitney?"

I snicker. "I haven't needed help to get onto a horse since I was ten."

"That doesn't surprise me. I can appreciate a strong independent woman," he replies with a wink.

We both get on the horses and slowly ride the outer track.

"So, *Animal Farm* . . ." he prompts once we get moving.

I exhale loudly, looking over at him. "I have a lot to say on the subject matter."

And really, I do.

We spend the next hour riding Ronald and Jeff, discussing the plot of the book, and the agony it's caused me. Our laughter echoes through the arena and more than once we end up bumping our horses into each other because we're too busy staring at each other.

Eventually we take a break from riding and have a seat on the old wooden fence.

Wyatt looks my way again, as if he's studying me.

"What?"

"I'm just trying to figure you out, you're so . . ." He shakes his head. "I can't figure out the word."

I feel my cheeks flush. "Is it something good at least?"

He flashes me another smile, though I'm convinced the guy never stops smiling. "Of course." And then his finger grazes mine and he says, "You're all-consuming, Whitney Harris."

Chapter 13

WYATT

Whitney's eyes are shining as she watches the horses roam around in the arena in front of us. We moved from sitting on the fence onto a bale of hay a while ago. I am so glad that she invited me out tonight and let me see this side of her. Watching her ride the horse was a core memory I'd like to keep in my mind forever.

It's like she and Ronald had their own secret language and I was quick to learn that Whitney would win in a race.

Every. Single. Time.

"So how many horses have middle-aged men's names?" I chuckle, nudging her shoulder.

"Well, there's Ronald and Jeff . . . Howard, Stewart. And then there's Kurt and Johnny Boy." She chews her lip, letting out a small giggle.

"How old were you and April when you named the horses?"

"Oh, twelve and thirteen." She gives me a coy smile and I laugh. "Scout embraced our name choices. What we didn't know was that when she died, the horses would be sold to Crystal and some of them would become racehorses. Ronald won the Kentucky Derby three years in a row."

"Wow, I didn't know I was with royalty, what about Jeff? Any big awards for her?"

Whitney pats my hand. "She's more of a homebody and a grass grazer."

We both turn to watch the horses again, two very different personalities showing up as they eat from the troughs—Jeff eating as if it's her last meal, and Ronald eating one piece at a time.

"Did she have other animals on the farm?" I ask suddenly, realizing an older woman might not have been able to tend to all the animals.

"No, she just had horses. The farm was passed down from her parents and she had a riding program set up with some of her friends, but April's mom got pregnant at fourteen and that took up a lot of Scout's time." She tells me with a sigh. "And then when April's mom started getting into drugs and risky behavior, Scout shut down the riding program. April's mom skipped town when April was seven."

I grab her hand because I honestly don't know what to say about it. I saw April for all of ten minutes at Scott's house, but I understand deeply how quickly April would have grown up in an environment like that.

And as I look at Whitney, my gut tells me that her situation would have been no different.

"You never talk about a grandfather, was Scout not married?"

Whitney crosses her legs and gives me a sad smile. "He was in the military, he never made it back from the war. But apparently, he was the kind of man who lit up the whole room when he smiled. Scout had a great group of neighbors and friends who adored her, so she had great support when raising her daughter alone and then when she took April in."

A heaviness fills my heart. My grandparents were not the best people so it made sense that my dad carried some of that into his marriage with my mom, but I struggle to understand how someone who was obviously well loved could turn around and blow up their entire life.

"Wow, sorry, that's a lot of heavy topics . . ." Whitney gives an abrupt laugh while looking at me nervously.

I give a shrug. "I like deep conversations. You learn more about people that way."

She nods her head slowly, chewing her inner cheek. I can sense her gears turning in her head.

"Thanks for coming with me, I haven't ridden a horse in a few months," Whitney says quietly from beside me.

"Why not?" I ask too quickly.

She turns to look at me and her eyes search mine. *Is she trying to figure out if I know she was attacked?*

"I just had some stuff going on . . ." She rolls her shoulders back and changes the subject. "What was your childhood like?"

She's deflecting, but maybe this will be a chance for her to open up to me about her life too. "I grew up in Nashville, my mom was a nurse at the hospital and my dad practiced law. My younger brother Wesley is almost ten years younger than me but he's smarter than most adults I know."

She's chewing on the inside of her cheek, as if she's trying to decide if there's something else she wants to ask me.

"I'm an open book, Whitney, ask me whatever it is you want to ask me," I say, shifting to face her.

"Did you have an easy childhood?" she asks timidly.

A harsh laugh escapes me before I can stop it and she jumps beside me. "Sorry . . ." I mumble, sighing. "It depends who you ask, but no. My dad was an abusive alcoholic."

Her eyes land on mine and I see understanding cross her face.

"My mom was too . . ." she whispers.

I don't force her to elaborate or share more, instead I pull her into my side and the two of us sit in silence for a while before she whispers, "I should get home, it's been a long week."

"I can drive you," I offer.

She nods silently as I reach for her shaky hand. I don't think Whitney tells people about her life often and I imagine her head is loud. I just want to know what other things she's spent her life suppressing.

She gives me the address but other than that, the drive is quiet beyond the radio.

When we finally pull onto the street, she speaks. "I'm sorry I ruined our date." Her voice is timid again, and it doesn't take an idiot to know that she's trying to put a wall up around herself.

My lips twitch as I say, "Our date, hmm?"

She's looking down at her feet, as I pull up to the house. "Our hang out?"

"Whitney, look at me."

She's clutching the door handle and I'm worried she's planning her escape. She hasn't unbuckled her seatbelt yet, so I still have time to not end the night like this, full of heaviness and discomfort.

"Whitney," I urge, trying to keep a soft tone.

She finally looks up at me. Her eyes look wet even in the dark. I want to hold her right now, take her walls down and build a new house around her heart.

"I'd rather we call it what it is . . . this is a date."

She closes her eyes and whispers, "*Focus on the wildflowers.*"

"Wildflowers?"

Her eyes snap open and she looks embarrassed. I grab her hand and she exhales. "Whenever I'm overwhelmed or upset, I tell myself to focus on the wildflowers. It's the people or moments that make you smile. It's something Scout taught me."

I let a sudden burst of boldness lead me as I kiss her knuckles. "I like that. I might need to steal that."

"Yeah . . . go ahead."

She gives me a half smile as she unbuckles her seatbelt, taking her hand from mine. "Night, Wyatt."

"Goodnight, Wildflower," I call out and the smile on her face shines brighter than the moon in the sky.

Goddamn, I'm going to fall in love with this girl.

Chapter 14

WHITNEY

Therapy was hard today, as I was reflecting on the first time Deacon hurt me and how emotionally confused I felt back then. How he manipulated me into thinking love was pain. I fell into the trap easily having been raised in a loveless home.

I really appreciate Dr. Boate because she lets me ramble from one topic to the next without interrupting me or expecting me to stay on task.

I walk down the main drag of Nashville, stopping outside Layla's Honky Tonk when I catch a familiar figure walking towards me.

"Whitney, hey," Wyatt says, stepping towards me, cautiously. He's dressed in jeans and a light blue T-shirt. A smile spreads across his face. "Fancy meeting you here."

For a moment, I forget about therapy. "Hi."

"How are you today?"

"Fine, you?"

"Good, thanks. Was thinking about getting some food. Would you like to join me?" He tilts his head towards the bar, and I shrug. There's no need to rush home, April and Kyle are away for a few days, so dinner was probably going to be a grilled cheese sandwich tonight.

"Sure." I nod, following him into the bar. Live music plays around us as we find a table near the back.

Wyatt looks over his menu as I take in my surroundings. I always order the same thing: the grilled chicken sandwich and fries.

"Howdy, folks, what can I getcha'?" A waitress appears beside me and my stomach sinks. "Ah, Whitney. It's been so long."

"Hi, Mrs. Frier." I keep my tone light, unsure how to address Deacon's mom. I didn't know she was working here.

"It's Darla, honey, you know that!" She laughs, before adding, "You look good, I was sorry to hear about what happened with your mom and Carl . . ." I stare at her with pleading eyes, knowing that Wyatt can hear what she's saying. "Everyone at the trai–never mind. It's just good to see ya, is all."

"Yeah. I'll have the chicken sandwich and water please," I say quickly, not looking at Wyatt.

"Right, of course." She finally senses my body language and then turns to Wyatt.

"I'll have the same please."

"Great. We'll get it started for you right away." She looks as if she wants to say more but thinks better of it.

I fidget with my fingers, letting my hair fall around my face as I try to calm my breathing, memories of the attack trying to fill my head. I try to channel what my therapist has taught me, but it all feels so far away right now.

"Hey . . ." Wyatt's voice is quiet and from the side of my eye, I see his hand sliding towards me. "What can I do?"

I shake my head, replying, "Just give me a second here." Rolling my shoulders back, I chew on my cheek. *This is so embarrassing—who has a panic attack in public, in front of the guy she sort of likes.*

Wait. I like Wyatt?

A giggle escapes my mouth as I stare down at his still outstretched hand.

Shit. When was the last time I liked a guy? I thought I loved Deacon when I was seventeen, sure, but ninety percent of our relationship stemmed from hatred and fear on my end.

I allow my hand to lay on top of Wyatt's, shifting my head up slowly until I find his eyes.

Worry fills his facial features, but he waits for me to speak.

"That was my ex's mom," I tell him quietly. He just nods and waits to see if I want to add more. "He wasn't good to me."

Wyatt's thumb brushes against mine.

A feeling fills my heart, like glass shattering, as I blink up at him. "Not many men have been good to me, Wyatt."

His voice is full of certainty as he says, "I don't want to be good to you Whitney, I want to be *great* to you. I want to help you see your worth."

My eyes widen at his words but when he leans forward and adds, "And from what I can tell so far, you are worth the world, Whitney Harris."

It's Sunday night when Wyatt invites me to "the best restaurant in town" which turns out to be his house.

Ellie and April assure me that I'll be safe and that they'll be on standby with mace and pitchforks just in case. I groan at their cheesiness, but I can't deny I appreciate their support and protectiveness.

Wyatt's house is a bungalow with a cute white picket fence. It's a lot of light wood tones and light blue. It's soft and calming, kind of like the vibes Wyatt gives out. I love it.

I stop in the front hallway, eyeing his family photos. "This is your mom and Wesley, I assume?"

He walks over to me and smiles, as if he appreciates me remembering their names. "Yeah. This was last Christmas, and this was Christmas seven years ago." He points between the two pictures.

My stomach knots. The two pictures hanging side by side are night and day. In the one seven years ago, smiles seem hollow and don't reach their eyes and both Wyatt and his mother have their arms wrapped around his brother, as if they're trying to protect him. The one from last year shows them all smiling with their full faces, crinkly eyes, shoulders relaxed, and Wyatt's mom looks younger than in the photos from seven years before. As if she aged in reverse.

"My old man died six years ago—liver failure from drinking. It was the best day of my life, theirs too, probably. My mom is a whole new woman, and my brother is thriving," he says slowly.

"Do you wish they still lived in Nashville?" I ask, moving further into his house, following him into his kitchen.

"Sometimes. But I think my mom needed a clean break. I visit them once a month and vice versa, and call her weekly."

"I had a step-sister. Sort of. It was only for a year, I guess—from my mom's second marriage. When my stepdad got arrested, she skipped town. We didn't get along, but I sometimes like to think that she broke the cycle and is happily married with kids somewhere."

His face mirrors mine—sullen and broken.

"How many times has your mom been married?" he asks, taking a pan out of the cupboard.

"Legally . . . two? But she had a Vegas ceremony with a man she met three days prior. I think they lasted a week after that. And she's had a steady stream of boyfriends over the years."

"Was there ever any man that wasn't . . . completely terrible?" Wyatt pulls cheese out of the fridge and eyes me.

I chew on the side of my cheek and shake my head. "None that ever paid much attention to me. Part of why I moved out is because one of her boyfriends would try to break into my room and play dumb about it."

Wyatt's eyebrows furrow and anger crosses his face. "I couldn't imagine . . ."

I sit down at his island. "Was your dad abusive before your mom married him? Or . . ."

Wyatt reaches a hand across to me and I place my hand in his. His finger rubs along my pinky. "She doesn't like to talk about it, but it felt like it got worse as I got older. He was a lawyer and worked long hours from the day I was born, but I feel like the drinking started when I was four or five. We went from always seeing my cousins and grandparents to not being allowed to have friends over."

"We're kind of sad, aren't we?" I assess.

Wyatt shakes his head, but his eyes still hold sadness. "No. Resilient is a better word."

Resilient. I think that's the perfect word choice.

"So, are you a fan of grilled cheese sandwiches?"

Do I breathe?

"Yes. They're my favorite . . . as long as there are—" My words trail off as he pulls a jar of pickles out of the fridge.

"Pickles?" he finishes for me.

"Yes!" I can't help but smile, and my smile grows all the more when he places a jar of pickles onto the counter in front of me.

Wyatt starts the grilled cheese for us, humming under his breath.

I find myself admiring him, not just for his body, but his heart. Something about him is so peaceful.

"Are you okay?" he asks me, nervously, and I realize I've zoned out, my eyes glued to his stomach.

I let out a long exhale, looking down at my lap. "Yeah. Sorry, I just zoned out."

"Can I ask you something?"

I nod slowly.

"What happened with your mom . . ."

I close my eyes, a hollow, "Which time?" falling from my lips, before I shake my head. "Did Ellie tell you something?"

"Not outright, but if you haven't noticed by now, I'm kind of observant. And your ex's mom made that comment . . ." He half smiles as he flips a sandwich into the pan. "You don't have to tell me if you don't want to."

"I don't think we have enough hours in the day to break down my life . . . but a few months ago her boyfriend attacked me, and I ended up in the hospital for a few days." I downplay it, adding a shrug to my movement. "I've been living with my best friend April and have a restraining order against my mom now."

"I'm so sorry . . ." Wyatt frowns.

"I hate to say the cliché, 'I'm used to it,' but I am."

"That doesn't mean you deserve it." he says, turning towards the stove top.

I purse my lips. "I know . . . Honestly, if I didn't have April and Ellie, I probably would have gone home and let it happen all over again."

Wyatt places a grilled cheese in front of me, with pickles on the side, before sitting beside me with a sad expression. "I'm glad you didn't . . ."

"Me too." I look down at my sandwich before taking a bite of it. It smells good and it tastes even better. "This is so good. Scout always said grilled cheese, pancakes, and wildflowers fixed everything. And most of the time it was true."

Wyatt half smiles. "Well, if you ever need a grilled cheese sandwich, you know where to find me."

"Thank you, Wyatt." I look up at him, hoping he realizes I'm not just talking about the sandwich.

He offers me a small smile as we both continue to eat. Over dinner he tells me a bit more about his mom and brother while I tell him more about April and Scout. Occasionally one of us will make a comment about things that broke us as children. It's strange, having someone understand my past so well without ever stepping foot into my shoes. April watched everything play out, but this feels almost as raw and intimate.

Somehow Wyatt feels like a secondary therapist to me, a damn good looking one who I sometimes feel the urge to kiss. But it's not clinical or one-sided, and part of me feels like I'm healing pieces of him too.

We talk for hours before he turns to me and says, "So, listen . . . It's late, and I know you said April is away, but if you want to stay here, you can. I don't mean it in a *sleep with me* way . . . I'll sleep on the couch; you can have the bed. I just want to know that you're . . ." He scratches his neck.

"Safe," I finish for him.

He nods slowly, avoiding my eyes.

"I appreciate the offer. Are you sure?" I move my crust around the plate.

"Yes. I'm sure. Let me just clean my room real quick."

I give him a small smile. "Wyatt, I basically grew up in a crack house and my mom's a hoarder—I'm used to a bit of a mess."

"Fair enough." He stands up and points towards his room. "It's this way. I'm just going to steal one of the pillows, if that's okay?"

"Take however many you need, it's your house Wyatt," I respond self-consciously, following him down the hallway.

He turns a side lamp on, illuminating his room. His furniture is all light gray with a matching bed frame, blue plaid comforter, and the walls are dark blue. It's simple but cozy.

"There's a phone charger here. Window is open. Feel free to close it. Any questions?" he says quickly, reaching down to grab a pillow off the bed.

"Uh, could I maybe have a shirt or something . . . so I'm not sleeping in a dress?" I ask with a nervous laugh.

"Yeah, of course." He opens a drawer and hands me a concert T-shirt. "Anything else?"

I shake my head. "No, I should be okay."

He steps back from me, nodding. "Okay. Night, Whitney."

I reach out to hug him, shocking both of us. "Hey . . . thank you, again. For everything."

"Anytime, Whitney," he whispers against the top of my head before stepping backwards and I swear I hear him sigh from down the hallway as I close the door.

I quickly throw the shirt on, crawling into bed. The sheets are so soft, and the bed is far more comfortable than the rickety mattress I grew up sleeping on. I don't mind April's guest bed, but something about this one feels fresh. *Homey.*

I turn the lamp off and plug my phone into the charger before my eyes close. I feel like I'm lying in a hug. But before sleep consumes me, my mom's voice fills my head, as it always does in the darkness.

Don't get too comfortable. You're not worth a thing to anyone.

My stomach sinks. No matter how much Wyatt makes me feel like I'm worth something, a part of me will always worry that he's going to break me too.

Chapter 15

WHITNEY

I wake up to someone shaking me and I scream.

"It's Wyatt!" he exclaims as I swat him away.

I open my eyes, letting myself remember where I am. "Oh . . . shit . . . s-sorry." My face is wet with tears and I'm in a cold sweat.

Nightmares, reality . . . it's hard to know the difference sometimes.

"You were calling and crying out in your sleep. A nightmare I imagine," he says slowly.

"I seem to have those from time to time," I whisper, sitting up and pulling my sticky hair off my face.

"You have a mean right hook. Remind me to not try and wake you from nightmares again." He chuckles. I turn to look at him and gasp.

He's shirtless, only a pair of boxers covering his body and his rock-hard stomach is on full display to me, evident even in the darkness of the room.

Seriously, you just had a nightmare about your mom and you're checking Wyatt out? Classy, Whitney.

"What?" He looks down at himself, as if to check if he has something on his stomach.

"I was checking you out, okay?" I groan, covering my eyes.

"Oh." I hear the smile in his voice.

Ugh, change the subject before you make it weirder . . .

"What time is it?" I ask.

"Just after four."

"Have you slept?" I ask, yawning, unable to look away from his ripped stomach.

"Truthfully, no. Having a gorgeous girl down the hall in my bed, is distracting my ability to fall asleep," he says honestly, a smile playing on his lips.

I fight back my smile. "Would it be easier if you lay beside me. Or will it be harder?"

He chuckles again. "Oh, definitely harder. *Much* harder."

"Wyatt! You're such a guy." I giggle, patting the bed beside me. "Come on then."

"I was just being honest, Whitney. But I made you laugh, so that's a bonus." His voice is husky as he slides under the covers. "Besides, I don't lie."

We both lie on our backs.

"Do you want to talk about your nightmare?" he asks me, his tone cautious.

I shouldn't be surprised at him at this point, he's always gentle and trying to check on me but the question catches me off guard. Deacon used to wake me up from my nightmares and expect me to repay him for disrupting his sleep.

I swallow a breath I didn't realize I was holding in, "N-not r-really. Sorry."

His pinky grazes mine. "I used to have really bad nightmares all the time. Relive everything I could have done differently to protect my mom and Wes. I hated sleeping, especially because he'd come home late, and I never knew if he would try something with my mom or I. I'd force myself to stay awake half the night so by the time I slept I'd be too tired to dream," he offers, and I know he's doing his best to make this feel like a safe space and make me feel like I can open up to him.

"You don't have nightmares anymore?" I close my eyes. *Maybe there's hope for me yet.*

I feel his body shift in the bed beside me. "There's the rare night that one will come, usually around my dad's birthday or the memories that haunt me the most. But most of the time, I'm okay. Therapy helped me, thankfully." Again, his pinky grazes mine, but I think it's to help him stay calm. I don't miss the anger in his tone.

"I'm going to therapy," I admit to him, feeling vulnerable. "It's hard to relive the worst moments of my life . . . but it's nice to share my story with someone else. It makes me feel validated."

He links his fingers through mine. "That's really brave of you, Whitney. You should feel so proud of yourself. It's a big step . . . and a hard one to take."

I squeeze his hand with mine. "My worst recurring nightmare is from when I was five or six. My mom was high on god knows what, and she brought some man home that started hitting her, and for some dumb reason I tried to protect her and he threw me off of her, causing me to hit my head. But the worst part is that my mom started laughing while I cried. I'd cut my head on broken glass and needed stitches."

His shoulders sink beside me. "I wish I could take away all the pain you've been through, Whitney."

His words always seem to find a way to wrap themselves around my heart. I try to stabilize my own breathing as I whisper, "Wyatt?"

"Yes?"

"Where are your wildflowers?" I turn to face him.

He blinks, meeting my gaze. This feels so intimate, I've never had this before. Laying in bed talking to a guy. Deacon always told me, "Beds are for sleeping and fucking, Whitney."

"You are the wildflowers, Whitney."

My hand brushes the side of his face as I say, "Would you like to spoon me?"

He clears his throat and stutters out, "I d-don't think I can."

"Why not? *Oh.* It would be more like a *fork*?" I try to hold in my giggles.

"Yes," he coughs out.

I roll back onto my side, facing away from him and whisper, "Forks are better than spoons in my opinion."

Wyatt mutters a low, "Fuck," before wrapping himself around me.

"*Jesus,*" I whisper as his warmth engulfs me and his body molds against mine perfectly, the outline of his dick firm against my back.

"Problem?" he asks with genuine concern.

"None in the slightest," I whisper and even though my walls are down for him, insecurities sink in, and I let my past dictate my next words. "Would you like to touch me?" I blurt out.

I feel his body tense from behind me.

"I mean . . . y-you don't have to . . . sorry that was forward . . . I . . . s-sorry," I stammer, flinching . . . but then I realize the hit isn't going to come. I won't be punished for my word choice.

Wyatt responds by running his finger along the hem of the shirt I'm wearing. "Whitney," he exhales before sliding his hand into my shirt. "It would be my pleasure to touch you, but not like this, okay?" His warm hand draws circles around my belly button.

"What do you mean?" I whisper, feeling the need to recoil, to push him away.

He hugs me tighter, as if he can sense my thoughts. "I don't want to rush into something here. We've had some heavy conversations tonight and you had a nightmare. That's not the time for me to sweep in and have my way with you."

The words feel new to me . . . odd. "Oh."

"Whitney, I'm sorry if that hurts your feelings, or makes you feel like I'm not interested. Because I am. *Trust me*. But I also think you've been conditioned to think you're supposed to be someone's punching bag or live to please others. That's not how I work. I want *you* to be comfortable and know your worth. I respect you if you want me to touch you like that, Whitney. But please don't think you owe me something, or I expect sex just because I'm a man."

I turn to face him and his palm lands against my cheek, gently rubbing his thumb against my cheekbone. I hold in my breath.

"Are you okay?" His voice is strained.

"Yeah."

"You're a shitty liar, Whitney Harris," he says with a lopsided smile as his eyes flutter closed.

"You're the first guy to ever make me feel safe," I blurt out.

His eyes snap open again and the sadness is written across his face. "Oh, baby . . ."

My lip trembles as a single tear rolls down my cheek and I put a shaky hand on his face. "Please kiss me," I beg.

He shifts closer to me, crushing his lips against mine gently. It takes half a second to process that he did what I asked. Fireworks erupt around us as he cups my face. Our lips part enough to let our tongues dance around together. Our mouths seem to be in sync, knowing what comes next and how to respond to each other. It is, without a doubt.

the best kiss I've ever had in my life. When he pulls away from me, we're both panting and I'm smiling like a mad woman.

"Holy shit, you're a phenomenal kisser," Wyatt states.

"I was thinking the exact same thing about you."

Though, phenomenal seems like an understatement.

Silence hangs between us for a moment so I assume he's fallen asleep.

"I need to romance you, Whitney. Take you on another date or twelve . . . You're a girl worth wooing."

I blink at him in the darkness. "You really are a nice guy, aren't you?"

"Yes." His face grows serious as he kisses my forehead. "I'm going to unbreak you. I'm going to build you up."

Butterflies dance around in my stomach as I lean forward to kiss him, softer this time, "Okay. Let's sleep, my big fork." I turn away from him, and as if I've got a hold on him, he wraps his arms around my waist, chuckling.

The last thing I hear before sleep finds me is, "Night, my little wildflower."

Chapter 16

WYATT

Whitney is draped against my chest like the perfection she is. It makes my dick hard; it makes me want to call in sick and spend the day consumed in her. But I can't do that.

Duty calls so I slowly get out of bed. I admire her, hair strewn everywhere, trying to claim my bed as its own. Fighting every urge I have to kiss her forehead, I leave a note on the bedside table beside her phone before I head out the front door.

When I get to the property, I'm beyond grateful to see that one of my crew members has brought coffee and donuts for everyone.

I welcome the coffee with open arms as I lean against the half-built island in the kitchen. Today is going to be a long day, for no other reason than me forgetting my head and heart at home in my bed.

"You okay?" Grant asks me as he nudges me towards the living room for our morning check in before filming starts.

"I couldn't sleep last night." I yawn.

"No shit, you're a zombie this morning," Grant snorts out.

"Whitney stayed over."

"Ah, is that why you couldn't sleep?" he teases me then lets out a breath when I glare at him. "I'm kidding, I know the both of you well enough, you probably sat up talking, huh?"

"Yeah."

"She's warmed up to you quickly, I'd like to say I'm shocked, but I'm really not. It took her about six months to trust me." Grant chuckles, before adding, "It was a good thing she met Bree first."

I feel special, knowing that she's warming up to me easier than with most and my smile gives me away.

"If you break out into song, I'm outta here," Grant states, before adding, "But seriously, I think you two are good for each other. Maybe she'll make you less annoying."

I shove his shoulder. "Oh, shut up."

"I'm kidding . . . anyways, I'm happy for you both."

"Do I need to invite Bree out for wine to tell her how sappy you're being at eight in the morning?" I tease.

Grant smirks. "She'll hear about it over mac and cheese tonight. And she'd be the first to tell you, I'm nothing but sap—that's what won her over. Good try though."

"Damn, I'm jealous. I love mac and cheese!"

"Come over for dinner then," Grant offers.

"Awe, are you asking me on a date?" I pull my hand to my heart.

"Don't start. I have two annoying brothers to deal with, don't make me regret our friendship. I can invite Ellie and Scott instead."

"You'll never regret our friendship, don't pretend. We're soulmates, Grant." I flash him my million-dollar smile.

"Drink more coffee, you're sleep deprived and acting far stranger than I'm willing to deal with today." He snorts out before adding, "But seriously, you're coming to dinner tonight, no arguing."

I clap my hand on his back. "I'll bring wine for Bree, and face paint for the girls. I'll be on my best behavior for you, don't you worry."

"Alright friends, time to get to work," Ellie calls out from somewhere in the house and I pull my work gloves on, ready to get started.

We spend the better part of the morning working on landscaping. I keep finding myself replaying all of my interactions with Whitney and how far she's come in the short time I've known her, but also how much she is helping me. I didn't realize there was anything I still needed to heal from until she showed up, and somehow, she's helping me forgive the parts of myself that still hold regret.

I'm weeding the front garden when a laugh sounds from behind me.

"What?" I say, as sweat rolls down my face.

"I much prefer watching Ellie weed her emotions out, but this will do. What's bothering you?" Scott props himself on the lawn chair beside me.

"What makes you think I'm bothered?" I throw over my shoulder.

"Because you're weeding. Normally you'd be first in line to help lay out the patio stones.

"I'm starting to care about her."

Scott smirks. "And that's an issue because . . ."

I turn to face him. "It's not a problem for me, but I think she'll run or pull back and I don't know how I'll deal with that. The two of us are similar in a lot of ways but I worry that'll hinder our relationship. I want to tell her I don't want to see other people because I'm half convinced she assumes I'm not going to commit to her, but I'm worried she'll recoil . . . I dunno man, I haven't been this in my head about someone before."

Scott's face grows serious. "How many times did I offer you a job before you took it?"

I give him a look of confusion but say, "Eight?"

"Yup. But I believed in you, I believed you'd be a good addition to the team, no matter how stubborn you are." I raise my eyebrow at him and he points a finger at me. "Yes. I know . . . I'm stubborn too, I almost lost the girl of my dreams. Don't remind me. All I'm saying is you have to make her know her worth before she's willing to break down all her walls for you."

I smirk. "Has Ellie made you start watching dating shows with her?"

"No, I learned all of this from my mom's soap operas." Scott grins and the two of us laugh before Scott stands. "But seriously, go get the weed whacker, you're wasting time!"

I flip him off as he stands.

But as he moves towards the porch, he gives me a sad smile. "She deserves someone like you in her corner. Lay the foundation and hopefully everything else will fall into place."

I give him a small nod, hoping that he's right. "Thanks, man."

I run home to change out of my work clothes before heading to Grant's for dinner. As I walk into my room, I freeze.

She made my bed.

Military grade.

If I had a quarter, it would bounce fifteen times. And the shirt and shorts are folded perfectly, like they're meant to be on a shelf in a store. I'd think it was endearing if I didn't know that someone broke her enough to get to this point of her life.

If my mom hadn't made our beds like this while my dad was alive, I probably wouldn't think anything of it.

My heart sinks as I sit on the side of my bed.

How do I break down her walls? How do I make her okay enough to leave the bed unmade?

I at least had a mom who loved me fiercely and a brother who gave me strength to rise above, but as I think about her screaming out in her nightmare, how she was curled into a fetal position because nobody in her house protected her . . . it suffocates me.

I'm trying to be a protector for her, but the damage was done a long time before I showed up.

I worry I'm too late and I can't unbreak her.

I'm always too late. I couldn't protect my mom or brother.

I move towards the front hallway and look at the picture of Wes, Mom, and me seven years ago and I let a memory come back.

"Wesley, smile for fuck's sake," my dad snarls. "How dumb are you?"

I wrap my arms around my brother.

I hate holidays.

"Oh lovely, trying to protect your brother after you abandoned this family. Now that you're twenty and working some shitty job you think you're the man of the house, huh?" My dad steps towards us and my mom flinches. "You know what I found last night?" He looks me in the eyes, and I clench my jaw. "You trying to get your mom and brother out of this house, huh? Sending apartment listings? Offering to house them in your one-bedroom shoebox?" He takes a sip of scotch.

I hate the smell of scotch.

I hate that he still makes me feel small.

"Here's what we're going to do. You three are going to sit, smile, and take the fucking Christmas picture so we can send it to my mother, and then I'm going to bring out your special gifts."

My mom is trembling. I shouldn't have come. I'm making it worse for them.

"Now smile, or I'll show Wesley what a baseball bat feels like. You remember that day, Wyatt?"

My eyes burn, but like always, tears don't fall. I use this picture as a reminder that I failed my mom and Wesley, that I should have tried harder. Because that was the day Wesley almost died.

My phone rings and my shoulders relax. It's like she has a sixth sense for when the past tries to wrap itself around me.

"Hi, Mom."

Chapter 17

WHITNEY

I'm having a bad mental health day. Something about the rainy weather and yet another email informing me of an apartment I didn't get has me feeling blue. I've spent the past week going from one end of town to the next, looking at places. I'm starting to lose hope and I feel like I've overstayed my welcome with April and Kyle . . . no matter how many times they've told me otherwise.

I've opted to pick up some restaurant hostess shifts in the evenings to get myself further ahead. Just because I don't have to pay my mom's medical bills anymore, doesn't mean that the debt went away.

Wyatt has been great about checking in with me and filling my day with silly texts and sweet voice notes.

My phone rings and Wyatt's name pops up on my screen. "Hello?" I answer as I lock the front door.

"Hey, you. Are you ready to be wooed?" he replies excitedly.

I can't help but blush at the prospect of being wooed, but my heart still feels heavy right now. "I just might be!" I try to sound chipper.

"What's going on? You sound sad . . ." His tone shifts to worry.

"Just having a rough day."

The ping of a text coming through makes me jump, but thankfully it's only Paige.

"Can I do anything? Are you busy tonight?" he asks.

I chew the inside of my mouth. "Sorry, Wy, I don't think I'm up to it tonight. I'm working anyway."

"Wy? Ah, my sweet Whitney is giving me a nickname?"

I purse my lips together, feeling my cheeks redden. "I . . . I guess so. I'm sorry."

He chuckles. "Oh, don't apologize, I love it. It feels more personal. Anyways, can I pretty please, with a cherry on top, take you somewhere tonight?"

"I'm working until ten tonight."

"Okay, well I voted and I'm going to pick you up from work and you can't fight me on it." His tone is light and teasing but I know if I said no that he'd be okay with that.

I can't help but smile. "Really?"

"Yes, Whitney, you deserve a hug if you're having a bad day. But also, I've missed your hugs."

My heart flutters with butterflies.

"Okay."

I hear someone call out to Wyatt in the background.

"Sorry, I gotta get back to work! Later, gorgeous." I go to answer but he's already hung up.

It's busy all day and before I know it I've got less than an hour left before I'm done with work. I find myself checking the clock on the wall and constantly scanning the front windows to see if he's here yet.

I'm standing at the front with my coworker, Jasmine, when I see a familiar figure open the front door. He's got his hat on backwards like always and a lopsided smile as he nears me.

"What does a guy need to pay to get into a place like this?"

Jasmine stands a bit taller, licking her lips. "With a smile like that, nothing." She's flirting with him. I know her body language too well by now.

Wyatt gives her a small smile before turning towards me, his smile growing with every step he takes towards me. My heart screams in delight.

"Hi, Whit." He smirks and I take note of him shortening my name.

"Hi, *Wy.*" I give a shy smile.

"Ah, my apologies." Jasmine coughs out awkwardly. "Didn't realize you knew each other."

"It's okay, Jaz!" I laugh. "This is Wyatt."

"Nice to meet you, Wyatt. Welcome to The Diner!" she says.

Wyatt gives her a small smile. "Nice to meet you." He looks at me. "I'll wait out front for you, okay?"

I nod, trying to keep my composure.

He taps the podium and it's then that I notice he's got *To Kill a Mockingbird* in his hand.

"Damn he's hot *and* he reads," Jasmine whispers to me as he steps away. "Good for you, girl!"

I let out a laugh before turning to watch him exit the restaurant, his jeans hugging his ass perfectly.

He glances over his shoulder at me and winks before he disappears from my sight.

Jasmine nudges me. "Go home early, I've got this covered."

"Are you sure?" I reply quickly, looking between her and the front door.

"Yes, go, have fun. Live a little," she says, pushing me away from the podium. "You work too hard."

"Deal. See ya Monday night!"

"Enjoy your weekend off." She winks at me.

I head to the locker room to put on my leggings and flannel shirt.

Wyatt is sitting on the ground, leaning against the restaurant wall. He's very concentrated on his book—his eyebrows are furrowed as his eyes scan the page.

I kick his foot and his head snaps up, apologetically. "Good book?" I ask.

His eyes dance as he says, "Scout is up to no good. Was April's grandma a troublemaker?"

I bite my lip, memories flooding me. "She was her own person and didn't like people doubting her, but I wouldn't say she was trouble."

"What is your favorite memory with her?" he asks, placing a bookmark in his book before putting it in the crook of his armpit.

I think for a moment before answering him as we start to walk towards his truck. "When she tried to teach me to knit . . . it was the first time I ever saw her frustrated and impatient. Up until then a part of me thought she didn't let anything phase her . . . all the times I showed up with bru—" I shut my mouth, looking to the ground.

"She was your wildflowers for a long time, hm?" Wyatts pinky grazes mine.

I nod silently, feeling a heaviness in my chest.

Wyatt's pinky grazes mine again but this time his fingers link through mine and I look up at him.

"Want to talk about it?" he asks softly.

I shrug as we reach his truck. "Not really."

He opens the door for me. "Are you tired?"

I think about it. "Not yet. I'd say you have an hour or so to woo me."

He laughs, motioning for me to get into the truck teasingly. "Hurry up then. But first . . ."

He opens his arms wide and I fall into his chest easily, wrapping my arms around his waist and then his arms wrap around my body too.

"Did your day improve?" he asks, resting his head on my forehead.

I lean further into it. "It just got a whole lot better."

"I'm glad." A kiss lands on my forehead. "Alrighty, let's get out of here."

I poke the tip of his nose as I get into the passenger seat. He gently closes the door, and my eyes trail him as he rounds the front of the truck.

"It's not far," he says, putting the truck in drive. I dare not ask where "it" is, I'd like to be surprised by the wooing.

He drives us to the edge of town overlooking the river and puts his truck in park before looking over at me with a lopsided smile. "Coming?"

I hop out of the truck and follow him to the back. It's got blankets and pillows laid out in the back.

"Stargazing?" I ask, blushing.

"Something even better!" He lifts me up into the box of his truck with his strong hands and hops up beside me. "Get cozy." He lays back and I follow suit, laying shoulder to shoulder. "My mom used to bring Wes and I out here when things were rough at home. I used to wish on anything that resembled a shooting star . . . hoping it would fix everything."

My heart pinches at his words, and there's a faraway expression on his face as if he's deep in a memory.

"Do you know the constellations?" I ask him as we stare up at the twinkling sky.

"Not well. I couldn't tell you which shape is which, but Wes and I would always try and make shapes out in the stars like . . . hmm . . ." Wyatt points up at the sky, with a content smile. "There's a slice of pizza right there."

I squint up at the sky and laugh at what is a very misshapen piece of pizza, "This is a bit harder than making shapes out of clouds, but let's see if I can keep up." I scan the sky for a moment. "There's a dog."

Wyatt chuckles, "I'll give that to ya, though it looks more like a blob. Hm, there's a log."

I squint at the sky. "Oh, I found a heart." I squint at the sky before pointing my finger up.

"Did you pay the sky to make a heart shape for me?" Wyatt teases. "How romantic."

I smack his shoulder playfully and turn to face him. "Yes, I had a long talk with the moon. I paid top dollar for it!" I tell him.

We smile at each other for a long time, and I'm half convinced he's going to kiss me until he says, "Look up."

I watch the sky for a few seconds and gasp as a meteor shoots past. And then another. I've never seen a meteor shower like this before.

I've never had a date like this.

I've never known a man like *this* before.

"Wow." I'm afraid to blink, I'm afraid to miss a single second of this.

"Make a wish, Whitney," he whispers.

I stare up as another one shoots at us. That's easy, I wish life could always feel this way. Comfortable. *Stable*.

And as Wyatt links his fingers in mine another word pops in my head.

Romantic.

The sky returns to normal, and I feel Wyatt watching me. I look at him, overwhelmed with emotions as my heart bangs in my chest. "That was amazing," I whisper.

He rubs my chin with his thumb. "You're amazing."

I roll my eyes, but I can't stop beaming, "Don't be so cliché."

Wyatt's face breaks out in a mischievous grin.

My nose scrunches up as he sits up. "What?"

"Just for that. I'll be even more cliche." He quickly jumps over the side of the truck. I sit up in confusion, but he just leans his head on the side, smiling down at me. "I'll be right back!" He opens the back seat and comes back with a guitar in hand.

I cover my eyes, butterflies taking over my chest.

"Stoooopppppp," I exclaim, even though it's the last thing I want him to do. I'm smiling like a fool.

"Now, Whitney, you haven't even heard me play yet. I'm not that bad," he teases, hopping back in the truck beside me. "What's your favorite song?"

I bite my lip as I think about it. "'Play it Again' by Luke Bryan," I lie. I feel like the song was overplayed by all my friends in high school who begged their boyfriends to learn guitar for the sole purpose of serenading them. But it seems like a song someone would know if they really did know how to play the guitar.

Without asking another question, he adjusts the strings before he wiggles his fingers and strums as if the guitar is an extension of himself. I sit up in shock as his voice fills the empty space of the field. My arms are covered with goosebumps.

When he's done singing, my face is on fire and it takes me a minute before I can say, "Play that song for many girls out in this field?"

Please say no.

"No, just you." He looks me in the eye, and I can tell that he's telling the truth. "Now tell me your actual favorite song."

I swallow, he's called my bluff. I should have known better.

I look down as I say, "Yours." I see his wheels turning as he furrows his eyebrows, so I add, "It's by Russel Dickerson."

"Hmm. I don't know that one," he admits as he pulls out his phone to look up the chords.

He strums slowly as he reads over the chords once, humming under his breath.

"Can you sing it for me? The opening at least so I can get the melody?" he asks so innocently, as if this isn't an intimate moment that's making my heartbeat faster than any time before now. This song is on repeat in my head these days, the lyrics always making me think of Wyatt.

"Please?" he adds, pouting like a puppy dog.

I quickly cover my mouth as a snort sneaks out, embarrassing me . . . *Smooth, Whitney, real smooth*!

He smirks at me. "I love that sound."

I roll my shoulders back. "Okay fine . . . smooth talker. Don't laugh at my voice. I don't sing for just anyone."

I have butterflies in my stomach at the thought of singing with Wyatt, but in the back of my head I can't help but remember the time my mom slapped me for singing too loudly. *You have a terrible voice. Shut up and pass me my cigarettes.* I chew on my lip, closing my eyes.

"Hey," Wyatt whispers, making me open my eyes. "It's just you and me, Whit. Nothing and nobody else . . . okay?"

It's just you and me.

"Okay," I say firmly.

He starts to strum the guitar and I allow myself to sit up taller as I sing. My voice is shaky at first and I don't look at him, but after a few beats he's singing along with me and our voices blend together. For the first time in my life, it feels like the universe actually wants me to be happy.

When the song is over, he grazes his finger along my cheek. "You make me better than I was before . . ."

I blush, leaning forward to kiss him.

He sings me a few songs before I let out a yawn.

"Sorry . . ." I start, rubbing my eyes.

He brushes my hair out of my face. "It's late, you're allowed to be tired!"

I bite my lip, I don't want to go home but I also don't want him to think I'm trying to shack up with him.

"Whitney?" His voice interrupts my thoughts.

"Yes?"

"Can we have a second attempt at spooning . . . or forking?" he asks as he hops down from the back of the truck, extending a hand to me.

We both let out a long laugh.

"Sure!" I try to keep my voice casual but I'm genuinely excited.

"Also . . ."

"What?"

"Your voice might be one of my favorite sounds." The way he says it makes it feel like it's a promise.

"Hey, *Wy*?"

"Yes . . ." he replies, his eyes glued to mine

"I think your voice *is* my favorite sound," I whisper. His lips find mine and nothing has ever felt more right than this moment.

I wake up in Wyatt's bed, his arms slung over my waist, his bare chest warming my skin.

I pinch myself. "Ouch."

Okay not a dream.

"Did you just pinch yourself?" His voice is raspy as he chuckles.

"O-oh . . . maybe." I laugh awkwardly. Dammit. I turn to face him and my heart melts. His hair is messy, and his eyes are sparkling.

"I'm real," he teases me.

"You sure are," I say, nuzzling against the pillow, "What time is it?"

"Half past when I should make you breakfast. But almost eight." His tone is teasing.

"Oh. When did you wake up?" I say, realizing he smells like toothpaste.

"Uh, six. I never sleep past seven." He gives an awkward laugh, as if he didn't expect to get caught.

"You could have woken me up," I tell him, feeling bad that he stayed in bed all this extra time.

He shakes his head side to side. "I'm pretty sure the Woo King would tell me that letting you sleep in is a subtle woo."

I snort, raising an eyebrow at him, "Who the hell is the Woo King and what the hell is a 'subtle woo'?"

He gives me a slow smile, one that reaches his eyes. "A *subtle woo* is me letting you sleep in, weren't you listening."

I roll my eyes at him sitting up. "Hardy har," I say, fighting back my smile.

"Wow, that wasn't a wooing laugh."

"Wyatt . . . if you say 'woo' one more time, I'm going to smother you with a pillow!" I warn him, picking up the pillow from behind my head.

He chuckles, pulling me against him. "Hey, Whit . . ." He leans his mouth near my ear and whispers, "Woo." I push him away, tickling his side. He lets out a yelp of a laugh and so I tickle him again. He squirms around, gasping through his laughter.

I pull my hands back, letting him catch his breath.

"Dammit, woman. How dare you tickle me." He wipes a tear from his eye and I give a victorious smile. Wyatt repays me by tickling me.

As I wiggle around the bed, getting tangled in the sheets, I feel completely at ease. And then something else hits me like a bag of bricks. This is the first time in my life that I slept all night. No nightmares.

He rolls out of bed and stretches his arms above his head, his abs taunting me.

"Do you like scrambled eggs?" he asks me.

"Sure do," I reply.

"Super. You stay cozy, I'll call you when it's done." He leans down and kisses my forehead.

"Ah no, I'll come along." I pull the sheets off of me and follow him to the kitchen, opening a cupboard, being nosy.

"What are you looking for?" he asks me.

"Do you have flour, salt, and cinnamon?" I peek at him over my shoulder.

He gives a confused smile and then digs around in another cupboard finding me supplies.

"And bowls and measuring cups."

"What are we making?" he asks as he places the items on the counter.

I look up at him nervously. "Scout's famous cinnamon pancakes."

He puts everything on the counter for me and I start pouring by memory. April's grandma spent a lot of time teaching me how to cook and bake growing up, but my favorite thing she made was the cinnamon pancakes. Although, I did memorize most of the recipes she taught me. Wyatt watches me move around his kitchen and I turn to him. "Can you put some music on?" I ask.

He nods and hooks his phone up to a speaker, tapping his chin as if he is trying to decide on a good song. And then his fingers hover over his keyboard as he looks up over at me.

"What?" I ask as I open the bag of flour.

"This song reminds me of you," he offers before pressing play. "My Girl" by Dylan Scott plays through the speaker.

My girl.

Chapter 18

WYATT

We dance around the kitchen together between flipping pancakes and frying bacon. It feels so natural playing house with Whitney. My face hurts from smiling. I love how alive I feel when I'm with her.

When we sit down at the table together, she watches me anxiously as I cut into my pancake. Her eyebrows are pinched together as she chews on her inner cheek.

I give her a reassuring smile before biting into it.

My taste buds flood with instant satisfaction. I look into her eyes as I swallow. "These pancakes are incredible."

"Really?" Whitney's green eyes widen, as if she's surprised. "Scout always made them the best; she always found a way to use the perfect amount of cinnamon."

"I can't complain. They're delicious," I tell her, after chewing on another bite.

She eats slowly, looking up at me between bites of food, as if she's trying to process her thoughts.

"What?" I ask with a smile.

She rolls her shoulders back. "Do you have plans today?"

"Nope, you?"

"Nope," she echoes, smiling. "I'm off all weekend."

My smile spreads even further across my face. "Wonderful. What would you like to do today?"

"I'm fine with whatever you want. I just might want to run home to get new clothes."

"Yeah, that works, I can drive you."

Whitney fidgets with her hands.

"What's wrong?"

"April isn't home today. She's out of town for a gig but I'm hoping you two can have a more official meeting someday. She's really important to me."

I squeeze her hand. "I'd love to meet her properly, you name a time and a place, and I'll be there."

"Okay," she whispers.

We continue to eat, and I ask about all the other things Whitney used to bake with Scout and April. As conversation flows, splatterings of her childhood come out, but one thing is constant, the smile on her face when she talks about the farm.

After we clear the dishes, Whitney reaches up into the cupboard to put the flour back and my eyes land on her thighs. Whitney looks adorable in my shirt but every time she leans forward or bends down, I catch sight of all the little scars that line her legs, and it makes my heart break for her.

She tugs on the shirt a few times after catching me staring at her.

"Sorry. I know they're . . . not pretty to look at," she mumbles, taking a long breath.

"Hey, don't. I'm not looking because they bother me," I say quickly, reaching for her hand, while letting out a sigh. "I . . ." A lump forms in my throat and the words seem impossible to find.

Whitney gives me a sad smile and pulls herself against my body, tucking her head against my chest, her hand laying on my heart. "My ex beat me up pretty badly on the one-year anniversary of Scout's passing." She pauses, shaking her head, before continuing, "I'd spent the day with April and was a mess of emotions when I got home, I wouldn't stop crying and silly me expected him to hold me and hug me, but he didn't. He . . . he tried to force himself on me."

My heart constricts at her words as anger towards her ex fills my chest. I force a deep breath out, trying to calm myself down.

"He . . . he didn't have my consent. I was so lost, and I just recoiled afterwards. I let my mom and Deacon's voices fill my ears with every hateful thing they'd ever said to me and I just . . . snapped one day. I tried to convince myself that I was just trying to clean him off of me and rid myself of the memories of his hands on me. I don't think I was trying to kill myself; I just wanted the pain to stop and to erase everything."

"Oh, baby . . ." I wrap her tighter against me, not sure what to say to her.

"I told April everything the next day, and she spent the next few months trying to help me figure my life out and give me something to look forward to. I started volunteering at Crystal's horse farm. Being able to hang out with Ronald, Jeff, and all the horses made me feel connected to Scout. I tried so hard to set myself up for success and find happiness but . . ." Her voice breaks.

I rub her back, trying to put myself in her shoes. "You did the best you could. You're the best person I know. I've never met someone so resilient and kindhearted. You're such a fighter and I admire it so much."

Whitney squeezes me tighter. "I don't deserve you."

I can't help but chuckle. "Yes. You do."

I feel her shake her head against my chest.

"Don't make me tickle you until you believe me," I tease her.

She lets out a small laugh and pulls back to look in my eye. "Thank you for being so easy to talk to."

I tuck a strand of her hair behind her ear. "I'm glad you trust me, I know it's not easy for you to talk about. I am always here for you."

She tilts up towards me and kisses me, mumbling, "I'm so glad."

When she pulls back from me, her eyes are so full of life.

"I said it once, and I'll say it a million times: I'm going to unbreak you . . . I'm going to build you up, one brick at a time."

Chapter 19

WHITNEY

After a quiet morning together, Scott and Ellie invited us over for a game night at Scott's house. Wyatt dropped me off an hour ago so I could shower and get ready. I choose my outfit—a maxi dress paired with my jean jacket and low brown boots—and pack clothes for tomorrow because Wyatt asked me to stay over tonight.

As I'm zipping up my bag my phone buzzes. It's an unknown number.

"Hello?"

"Ms. Harris?" the female voice says on the other line.

I let out a sigh. "Y-yes, who is this?"

"This is Melanie Young, I'm a nurse at Nashville Grace Hospital, you're listed as the emergency contact for Ms. Karen Harris. She was just admitted to the hospital, and she says you're the person to contact about medical bills."

I blow out air. "Did she overdose?"

"I can't disclose that information over the phone," Melanie replies quickly.

"She's my mother, I used to pay her medical bills but that stopped a few months ago. There should be a legal document my lawyers can send to you," I reply quickly, logging onto the laptop April let me borrow so I can provide the contact information for both my lawyer and the case workers. I find the contact information and relay it all to her.

Melanie puts it into their system, and I send an email to my lawyer and case worker to keep them in the loop.

"So sorry to bother you," Melanie says quietly.

"It's alright, I know it takes time for paperwork to be processed . . ." I tell her softly.

"Thank you so much. We'll make sure to sort this out, so it doesn't happen again."

"She . . . she's okay though?" I ask, feeling a weight in my chest.

I know she doesn't need to tell me and truthfully, I don't know if I want to know. Melanie replies by saying, "We're taking good care of her. Nothing a good night's sleep won't fix."

I feel a sense of pride for not letting myself back pedal or offer to pay whatever medical expenses might take place, but a slight pang in my heart rises to the surface when I realize that no matter how much growth I'm doing, she still exists in the world.

Wyatt's truck pulls up to the house as I hang up the phone, I turn to look into the mirror and fake a smile.

Don't ruin tonight.

I lock up and head out to Wyatt's truck hoping he won't be able to read my body language or notice that my smile isn't meeting my eyes.

I get in and buckle up.

"Hey, gorgeous, I love your dress." He leans towards me, kissing my forehead.

"Thank you, it's one of my favorites. I have a few more still at my mom's place that I love . . . although, she's probably burned them or something by now."

"If you ever want to go get them, I'm happy to help."

That's the last place I want to go.

Especially right now.

Wyatt backs out of the driveway, and we head towards Scott's house with me filling the conversation with fluffy topics, hoping he can't tell that my mind is somewhere else.

When we park in front of Scott's house, Wyatt turns to me. "Did something happen? I don't know if I'm reading into things, but you seem to have a wall up right now. I know that seems crazy to say because you've been chatty, but your smile isn't reaching your eyes. Again, if I'm reading into things then I'm sorry . . ."

I turn to face him and sigh. "My mom is in the hospital. The paperwork should have been sent through by now to take me off the contact and payment form. I assume she overdosed. It just . . . caught me off guard. Her voice in my head has become far less frequent but I'm worried this will knock me back. I didn't want to tell you because I didn't want to ruin the night. I should have known you'd . . . be quick to figure it out," I say with a nervous laugh.

He squeezes my knee and asks, "I'm sorry, Whit. That's a lot to deal with. Can I do anything?"

I shake my head. "Honestly, no. I think a night with friends is exactly what I need right now. But if I change my mind, I'll let you know, okay?"

"You sure?" Wyatt says quietly, his eyes searching mine. "I love seeing how strong you're being, and I'm so proud of you . . . but I'm here. Got it?

I press a kiss to his cheek, feeling surprisingly calm. "I promise, Wy. I'm doing much better than I expected to be. Let's go have fun."

He thinks about it for a moment before opening his door. I meet him around the front of the truck, and he holds me against him for a long time before we head up the front path.

We knock on the door and Scott is quick to let us in. Even though I'd been here once before, I take in my surroundings differently this time, because I know everybody here and I know my environment. I stare around the living room at the design choices and try not to laugh when I see all the elm wood features. Scott catches me staring, "What can I say, I love me some Elm."

Ellie approaches with a laugh, giving me a tight hug. "Elm wood, Ellie Elm. Some Elm trees in the back, the man is borderline obsessed."

We move towards the living room where Paige is sitting with a few other crew members. I give a small wave to the guys as Paige stands to hug me. "Hey lady, I'm glad you're here."

"Me too. I love the hair," I tell her, pulling on the new pink streaks scattered within her dark curls.

Paige winks at me. "You know I like to change things up."

"How did your Nona feel about it?" I tease.

Paige pulls out her phone and scrolls to a picture of her, her mom, and her Nona all with pink streaks in their hair.

"No way!"

"I was worried my dad was going to pass out when he saw us. It was priceless. My Nona is going to try and convince her friends to hop on the trend."

She turns her phone to show everyone else the photo and I realize I didn't say hi to Grant, so I move towards him,

"Hi, sorry for getting to you last!" I say.

He gives me a big bear hug. "It's okay, I know I'm your favorite. How's it going, Whitney?"

Grant and Wyatt are similar in a lot of ways, they both have this overwhelming sense of calm and protectiveness.

"I'm hanging in there," I tell him. "How are my three favorite Thompson gals?"

"Good, Bree is taking them to a movie tonight. They got their Halloween costumes the other day. Chloe refused to take it off yesterday."

"Raising headstrong women, I love it!" Paige interjects as she passes us to sit down on the couch.

Wyatt sits on the couch beside me, handing me a glass of ginger-ale and then wrapping his arm around my shoulder. I don't miss how Ellie and Paige exchange smiles as they watch us, or the way Scott smirks at Grant.

We play a few different games together and I feel so at ease. It's so fun to see Ellie and Scott's competitiveness in full gear and Paige giving unhinged answers during Cards Against Humanity. But it's the way Wyatt and I seem to always choose each other's answers without realizing it—it's like our sense of humor and train of thoughts are interconnected.

"I feel like if we went on the *Newlywed Game* right now, you guys would kick our asses." Grant laughs.

Wyatt and I lock eyes and I feel warmth roll through me. I never expected someone to understand me so deeply.

I kind of love it.

Chapter 20

WYATT

Tonight was so special—seeing Whitney laugh, so carefree and at ease makes me so happy. And every time she leaned into me, or put her hand on my knee, or sang along to the song playing, I felt a part of her continuing to heal.

She spends the drive home rambling on about how fun tonight was and how happy she is to share moments like this with me. The giddiness and genuine smile on her face are contagious and it's almost as if the idea of her mom being in the hospital isn't nagging at her or weighing her down.

When we get into the house, she kisses me before looking up at me with her doe eyes. "Every single day I spend with you is better than the time before. I'm so lucky to have you, Wyatt."

I pull her into a long hug. "Not as lucky as me!"

She chuckles, poking my side. "We can agree to disagree."

I kiss her forehead. "I'm fine with that. Are you holding up okay? With your mom and such?"

She thinks about it for a moment before nodding. "I think so. I think I'm seeing her in a different light now, you know? Like, it's sad, but I also know that it's not my problem anymore . . . I can't let it be my problem."

She leans into me, and I rest my chin on top of her head. "It's hard to move forward, but you're doing so well."

Her voice is soft as she whispers, "I'm trying my hardest. Therapy has been helping and having you to lean on has been too."

We hold each other for a while before she lets out a long yawn, causing me to laugh, "Ready to move to bed, sleepyhead?"

She nods, pulling her bag up her shoulder, following me down the hall. She slips into the bathroom while I change out of my jeans and T-shirt, into a pair of boxers. The bathroom door opens, and Whitney calls out, "Brush your teeth with me?"

I go to join her, and my heart skips a beat as I take her in.

She's thrown her hair up into a messy bun and is wearing an oversized purple t-shirt. I pick up my toothbrush, facing the mirror—my eyes unable to leave her body—and her eyes stay trained on mine just the same.

"I don't hear her voice in my head as much anymore . . ." she says with a victorious smile as she puts a dollop of toothpaste on her brush, before handing the tube to me.

"And hopefully someday, it'll be a long-gone memory." I press a finger into her forehead. "Someday it'll feel like nobody broke you, and your head and your heart will feel truly healed."

Part of me wants to tell her that she also doesn't seem to have nightmares when she sleeps beside me, but I want her to come to those discoveries on her own.

"I feel like that day is coming sooner than I could have ever expected."

Neither of us speak for a moment, but when I see her eyes roam down in the mirror with a devilish smile, I know exactly what she's thinking. As soon as she spits out her toothpaste she leans back against my body.

When I place my toothbrush down on the counter and she turns to face me. "Hi."

"Hi, beautiful," I echo with a smile as I tilt my head towards the bedroom. "Shall we?"

She nods, following behind me. When we get into my room she turns to face me, her hands trailing across my chest again. "Wyatt . . ."

I tilt her chin up towards me. "Yes, baby?"

"I . . . uh . . . do you . . ." She lets out an awkward laugh before saying, "Can we have sex?"

I chuckle and she giggles nervously in response, biting her lip. "I didn't know if I was supposed to just jump your bones or just strip naked, I don't exactly know how to do this the 'normal way.' I just . . . I'm ready for this step with you and you just make me feel so . . . complete. I—" Whitney rambles but I cut her off by kissing her and lifting her into my arms. She wraps herself around me as our tongues dance together, creating the best kind of fireworks.

I lay her onto my bed and look down at her with furrowed eyebrows. "If I do anything you don't like, tell me, okay? I don't want you to be uncomfortable," I say softly.

Whitney nods, her green eyes shining as she places her hand on my cheek. "I trust you, Wyatt. With every fiber of my being."

I run a hand up her thigh, pulling the shirt up to expose her black silk underwear. Moving my hand across the top of the underwear, Whitney lets out an audible moan and her eyes shift back into her head.

Good Lord.

I'm watching her intently as I let my fingers dance across her skin, reading her cues, discovering her impatience. Seeing this side of her feels intimate in a much different way than I'm used to with her. It's as if we've stripped back another layer.

I'm sure she feels exposed and vulnerable; but I love knowing that she trusts me to touch her. I want my touch to erase every scar that other men have caused her over the years. I want her to know that her body is meant to be worshiped, not destroyed.

My fingers fall into her underwear and her legs spread in response, ever so slightly. She closes her eyes and a growl catches in my throat as my finger enters her, slick from her wetness.

I keep my movement slow, to let it linger. I doubt anyone ever gave her the attention she deserved, and I'm damn sure going to make sure she knows that this isn't about my pleasure.

This is all about her.

My own little wildflower.

When my thumb presses against her clit, she comes undone around my finger. I'm sure I look mighty proud of myself, but you can't blame a guy. It's instant gratification and it's made me hard as a rock.

Whitney looks up at me with glossy eyes. "That was the quickest orgasm I've ever had and by far the best. I don't even care if that goes to your head right now."

I chuckle, sliding her shirt up over her head. Whitney blushes as my eyes and hands explore every inch of her skin. I start to kiss my way up her stomach and a sigh of admiration leaves my lips. She tries to bring her arms across her body, and I see a flicker of panic in her eyes.

"Whitney . . . look at me," I say with a serious tone, willing her to move her arms. "You are a *fucking goddess*."

Her arms fall from her body, and she runs her hand through my hair. "What did I do to deserve you?"

"You looked up at me with these bright green eyes, that's what you did. That's all it took to make me a goner." I smirk before bringing my lips back to hers.

I cannot get enough of her.

I move back down her body, trailing kisses as I go and when I reach her inner thighs, she lets out a squeal. "Ticklish?" I ask teasingly, kissing her inner thigh again.

She squirms in response.

"Gorgeous, stay still. *Please.*"

I watch her cover her mouth as my tongue finds her center. The taste of her is making me feel insatiable . . . as if this is my first meal. Or my last. I eat her out like she's a hot fudge sundae, making her come undone over and over again until Whitney finally shoves my head away from her as she pants loudly.

"You okay?" I ask, thinking that she's overwhelmed and needs to stop, but she gives me a content smile.

"Yeah . . . I just need five seconds to catch my breath," she breathes out, placing her hand on my forehead.

"You sure?"

"Yes, Wy. I'm positive. But you can stop if you don't want to do it anymore," she replies, a nervous smile on her lips.

"Oh, trust me, baby, I wasn't done," I say, resting my head on her leg with a mischievous smile.

"Oh, okay . . . carry on then," she tells me with a playful laugh.

"At your service." I wink before returning my head between her legs.

Whitney is squirming and it sounds like she's trying to speak but her words keep catching on the rolling orgasm she's having. Her hands clutch at my hair and every time she seems to be trying to push my head away, she changes her mind at the last minute, pulling me deeper against her.

Suddenly she yells, "Apricot!"

I pull back from her with amusement. Chuckling, I ask, "Did you just say *apricot*?"

"Y-yeah . . . I need you to st-stop so I can catch m-my breath . . ." she pleads, closing her eyes, her chest rising and falling frantically.

I can't help but smirk. "Apricot, huh? Weird safe word but I'll accept it."

"It was the first word that came to mind . . ." She laughs, a playful smile on her lips. "Blame the apricot soap you have in the bathroom."

"Well, it's unique and I think it should stick." I meet her eyes and her eyes fill with appreciation. "You *apricot* me and I stop, no matter what. I promise."

"Thank you," she whispers with a cheshire cat smile. "Now take your boxers off!"

I stand up beside the bed but before I can pull my waistband down, Whitney pulls me towards her. My boxers do little to hide my excitement, especially once she slides the waistband down. I spring out towards her like she's a beacon guiding me home.

Whitney bites her lip, looking up at me through her eyelashes and mumbles, "Jesus Christ, Wyatt Morgan."

"You okay?" I ask, about to offer that we can take things slow, but my words are cut off by her mouth wrapping around my dick. "*Fuck,* Whitney," I groan, watching her move my length in and out of her mouth. She licks my tip and looks up at me again with lust in her eyes.

I reach into my bedside table beside me for a condom and roll it on at record speed before positioning myself over her on the bed.

"Are you sure this is okay?" I offer.

I look at her and she gives me a reassuring nod before I slowly ease myself into her. She squeaks out, her arms circling my shoulders as I move my hips slowly, letting both of us adjust to the feeling.

Whitney closes her eyes as I shift my body against hers and a part of me worries she's trying to hide or she's uncomfortable. But when she opens her eyes and they lock on mine, a wave of something moves through me.

Love.

"Wyatt," she says quietly as my pace quickens, her eyes glossing over.

"I'm right here, baby. It's just you and me."

And as if we are truly in sync, we both mumble out, "You are my wildflower," before coming apart together.

Chapter 21

WHITNEY

The week passes slowly for me, Wyatt is working late hours and so am I, so we haven't seen each other since last Sunday. After we slept together, something shifted. We spent most of Sunday touching each other. I'd never been able to look at anyone during sex before, but also nobody had ever made it about me and my pleasure before. Being able to look into Wyatt's eyes—seeing his endearing gaze was enough to make me come undone.

It made me feel loveable.

The days are getting cooler, and leaves are starting to fall from the trees, making me feel at peace.

Last night in therapy I talked to Dr. Boate about Wyatt and how we had sex. It was weird telling a middle-aged woman about my sex life, but it felt important to share . . . I could only compare it to the sex I had with Deacon, but it felt like night and day. I felt like it was for me for once, like my body was a delicate flower instead or something to rip to shreds.

April nudges my shoulder, bringing me out of my thoughts. "Are you in la la land?"

"Kind of, yeah." I turn my attention back to the fabric wall, catching sight of fabric covered with grilled cheese print.

"Would it be weird to make a grilled cheese blanket for myself?" I ask, half-jokingly.

"No, I think it would be weirder if my grilled-cheese-obsessed-best-friend *didn't* buy that fabric . . ."

"If you insist . . ."

I grab the fabric off the shelf excitedly and then stop to look at the sewing machines on display. I want to buy one someday, but I want something old school and vintage like the one Scout owned.

We're checking out at the cash register when my phone buzzes.

Wyatt: Hello, my wildflower. What are you up to this evening?

Whitney: Nothing yet. You?

Wyatt: Wanna come to a hockey game with me and some of my oldest friends? April can come too, finally get more than a quick wave?

I bite my lip. *I love hockey.* But it's the second part of the text that makes me smile. He wants me to meet his friends—not just Ellie and Scott's crew, but people from his childhood.

Whitney: April has a performance tonight, but you can count me in. Where should I meet you?

Wyatt: I can pick you up if you want, or you can come here, your call.

Whitney: I'm fine to head to your place, save you a drive in the wrong direction.

Wyatt: Yeah, cool. Come by around 3:30?

Whitney: Deal. See you then.

"Wyatt?" April asks with a knowing smile.

"He wants me to meet some of his friends tonight," I tell her, chewing the inside of my cheek.

"This seems unfair. He's spent all of ten minutes with me." She nudges my arm playfully as we move outside.

I give her a side hug, "It's not my fault you're taking off in the music scene and have performances most nights I'm not working. Hopefully soon." And truthfully, I do want them to meet properly soon. It's been months of trying to coordinate schedules.

"I'm really happy for you, Whit. I know there's still some things we need to figure out for you but seeing you stand a bit taller and knowing you're worthy of someone's attention feels nice." She fidgets with her shopping bags. "I hope you're really letting yourself feel everything in full and not getting into your head."

"I'm trying my best, April." I exhale slowly. "Therapy has helped and working at a job I love is nice. Day by day I'm feeling stronger."

"Man, remember when Scout brought us to a baseball game, and she caught a ball for us and made a few members of the team sign it." April gets a faraway expression as we reach her car.

"Oh gosh, and there was that super hot player who waved at us, and we both freaked out!"

We both laugh and spend the whole drive home talking about all the good times with Scout.

We park and April turns to me with a frown.

"What?"

April chews her lip before telling me, "I wanted to take your place, I wanted you to be at the farm with her so I could carry the pain. I don't remember my parents much; I don't remember what they did to me, but I remember every single time you showed up . . . whether because of your mom, the man she was seeing at the time, or Deacon . . . I just want that part of your life to disappear."

A tear trickles down her face as some brim in my eyes too. "April, I made it out, okay? I made it here because of *you*."

"I just hope that ten years from now it's such a distant memory that you never flinch." April is sobbing as she rambles.

"Hey, don't cry, it'll get me going too," I say, blinking back my own tears. "I'm not going to sit here and say I appreciate the struggle, or that it made me stronger because it didn't. *You* did. Scout did. Ellie did too. And at the end of the day, I wouldn't be here without you. I will never be able to repay you for everything you've done for me. Maybe my mother wasn't the best family, but you sure are." I pull her against me.

"I love you," she whispers. "Scout is beaming down from heaven at you, you know that right?"

"She's beaming at both of us," I reply, squeezing her tighter.

April wipes her eyes and sniffles. "Now, let's go start on your blanket before you have to get ready for your hot date!"

"Deal." I open the car door, following her into the house, ready to let my fingers work their magic with the sewing machine and help us connect with Scout's memory.

April and I work together for a few hours before I have to get ready for the hockey game.

I shower, paint my nails blue, and pull on my Nashville Predators jersey, before throwing on some jeans, and leaving my hair down.

"Damn. You just need one more thing!" She rummages through my make-up bag, pulling out bright red lipstick.

If Wyatt's jaw doesn't fall onto the ground, I'll be utterly disappointed.

"Ready to go?" she asks. "I can drive you on the way to Bluebird Cafe."

"Sounds good!"

We make the short drive before exchanging another long hug.

"Sisters forever," I tell her as I step out of her car.

"Sisters forever," she promises.

I ring his doorbell at exactly 3:30 PM. He's on the phone when he opens the door. His eyes zigzag over my body and he leans against the door frame, a sheepish smile on his lips.

It's not hard to focus on the wildflowers when he looks at me like that.

"Yeah, sounds good, man. We'll see y'all in a bit!" he says into the phone before slipping it into his pocket.

"Holy hell, Whitney. You're stunning!" He pulls me into a hug and the smell of the ocean fills my lungs. His heart is pounding out of his chest, and I'm instantly calmed by his presence. "How am I supposed to pay attention to the game with you looking so . . . delectable?" he stammers.

I shrug, a smirk playing across my lips. "I can go home and change."

"Absolutely not!" he exclaims with a laugh. "Come on in, I just need to grab my wallet and my hat."

I hang out by the front door but Wyatt yells from down the hall, "If I kiss you, will my lips turn red?"

I let out a small laugh before calling out, "Maybe."

He emerges. "Oh well, better to find out before we get there, isn't it?" he says, filling the space between us with three long strides. His one hand cups my jaw, pulling my mouth up to his and I moan as his warm breath tangles with mine. The kiss is slow, thoughtful. When he pulls back, a slight pink stain on his lips.

"It's like a lip stain," I comment, wiping his lips, thankful that it comes off easily.

He chuckles. "At least I didn't ruin yours." He pulls his hat backwards and I feel my knees buckle a bit.

God, he's sexy.

He wiggles his eyebrows at me and says, "Ready to meet some of my favorite people?"

"Heck, yeah!" I respond, moving so he can open the door.

We get to the stadium, and like always, it's crowded, and fans are excited. I love watching people's joy, seeing people have so much passion for something. Wyatt slings his arm over my shoulder casually, as if its an old habit.

I don't know if he realizes it makes me feel so protected, so secure.

He leads us towards the ticket line. The guy working gives him a nod and ushers us through. We walk through the crowd, his hand on my lower back guiding me forward. I see him scan the crowd.

"Over this way." He steers me towards a group of three guys.

"'Sup loser!" One of the guys calls out to Wyatt, before grabbing him into a hug. "*Oh.* Who's this?" His brown eyes find mine.

Wyatt stretches his arms out as if he was showing me off. "This is Whitney. Whitney, this is Frankie, Austin, and Mark."

I extend my hand to each of them. "Nice to meet y'all." I smile, taking them in. The three of them wear friendly smiles on each of their faces.

They instantly feel like a safe space.

Mark taps his chin, sizing me up. "So, Whitney, do you like hockey?"

All of them look at me, waiting for an answer.

"Damn right I do . . . I love that it's split into quarters, and they get touch downs. It's pretty impressive, don'tcha think . . . especially since they wear skates on grass!" I twirl my hair between my fingers and flutter my eyelashes.

Wyatt lets out a howl of laughter and Austin and Frankie both join in.

Mark looks completely amused.

I smirk at Mark. "If you sit beside me, maybe I can keep you up to date on all the stats for the team. My best friend's cousin is on the team. If April wasn't working tonight, she could have introduced you to him."

Mark looks at Wyatt, shaking his head in amusement. "Damn, why have you been hiding her away from us."

Wyatt pats Mark on the back. "Sorry, you can't keep up with the cool kids."

"Alright everybody, let's head to our seats," Austin chirps in, looking at his watch before adding, "Mark's buying the first round."

Frankie falls into step with me as Wyatt, Austin, and Mark talk two steps ahead of us.

I observe the three of them as they talk animatedly.

"So you're the gal that's been keeping Wyatt out of trouble, huh?" Frankie says.

I let out a laugh.

Is that *what I am? His gal?*

"I guess I am."

"Well, it's really nice to finally meet you . . . not sure why you stuck around after he bought you *Animal Farm*."

I smirk, "He told you?"

"Oh, yeah . . . we gave him a hard time about it for a few weeks, I think that's why he was worried about introducing us to you."

"It's okay, my best friend had a good laugh about it when I painstakingly tried to read it," I reply before asking, "So, y'all grew up together, yeah?"

"Yeah, we've been inseparable since kindergarten. Wyatt protected Austin from the class bully. Mark and I were quick to stand beside him, and we've just kind of never left it since."

"Ah." I nod. *His own version of April.*

"He's a good guy," Frankie tells me, as if I didn't know that already.

"Yeah, too nice sometimes," I joke.

Frankie snorts and Wyatt looks over his shoulder at us, the most subtle flicker of concern in his eyes. "What?" he asks.

Frankie smirks at him, "She said you're too nice sometimes."

Wyatt stops walking, tilting his head to the side, a glimmer to his caramel eyes, and my heart tightens with a feeling I can't place. "Is that so?"

"Y-yeah . . ." I stammer, blushing.

"Well, good reminder for everyone that the good guys are capable of making the ladies blush." He winks at me. "Carry on, tell him how nice I am," he teases, his tone full of amusement before turning back to Austin and Mark.

Frankie snickers, "You're in trouble now."

I roll my shoulders back as I stifle a laugh, it's refreshing knowing that me being "in trouble" won't end up with me getting beaten or yelled at. I watch Wyatt's profile as he moves ahead of us.

I've never known someone so gentle.

Frankie asks me a bunch of questions about myself, almost in a rapid-fire succession. "Gee, sorry I probably seem nosy or protective." He gives me an apologetic smile, shrugging.

I shake my head. "No . . . you're just being a good friend, trying to learn about the girl your best friend has been hanging out with."

Frankie smiles at me. "You're Wyatt's wildcard, aren't you?"

A quiet laugh falls from my lips. "His wildcard?"

"Yeah, to be a cliché sports fan, you're the hat trick nobody expected, the sudden seven-point lead in the last period." He shrugs. "The kind of girl who he deserves."

I hug my arms around my waist and look at Frankie, "I don't deserve him."

Frankie chuckles, slapping my shoulder like we're old buddies. "Oh, if you're saying that, then you deserve him all the more."

We come to the top of the stairs and the guys lead us right behind the penalty box. I gawk as they sit down. Wyatt pats the seat beside him with a silly smile, as he takes in my giddiness.

"Come on then, before we kick you out of the club," Austin jokes.

I sit down beside Wyatt. "What club?"

"The Nashville Hockey Fanclub, obviously," Mark throws out.

"Jokes on you guys, I can check out all the soccer players from here," I tease, giving a devilish grin.

Wyatt leans into me. "God, you just keep getting better."

"Whitney, do you drink beer? Or are you more of a fruity cocktail gal?" Mark asks.

"Just water," I say with a small smile, but Wyatt's finger grazes mine. "Actually, lemonade will do. Thanks."

"Make that two." Wyatt nods in agreement, linking my fingers through his.

"Okay, five lemonades it is," Mark jokes as he walks past us. "And Whitney?" I look in his direction. "Welcome to our club," he says with a nod.

Chapter 22

WYATT

I didn't know what to expect from Whitney tonight, but she was just as invested in the game as the guys and me. When she runs to the bathroom the three of them look at me with wide smiles.

"Damn, dude. Your mom is going to love her." Austin laughs.

"Yeah, she's eager to meet Whitney, but I figured I'd ease her in with you guys first." I shrug. My mom has been after me to bring her every time I visit now, but I don't want to overwhelm Whitney, especially since she and my mom are alike in a lot of ways.

"I know you don't need my approval, but you've got it," Mark adds in. "Especially since the Predators are ahead right now, she might be a good luck charm for us."

We all chuckle. Most games we attend end in a loss and it's currently 4-0. Whitney comes back down the steps, with her hands full of popcorn containers. "Here ya go, y'all." She turns back to face the rink. "What did I miss?"

I fill her in, and we settle against our seats, turning our attention back to the game.

After the hockey game, our normal tradition is to go out for wings and beers and I'm worried Whitney will just want to go home. I'm asking a lot from her to be out with my friends all evening.

I love spending time with her, but I also worry she won't appreciate how much time I actually spend with my friends. It's been an issue in previous relationships, but my friends are my family and I refuse to lose that.

But Whitney is different. I'm learning that more and more every day. She understands having chosen family and apparently, she loves wings more than me and the guys do.

When we order drinks, she orders a beer and I give her a confused expression and she mouths "safe space." Knowing that she feels safe with my friends makes me happier than she'll ever know.

Another reminder that she just might be perfect for me.

Whitney and Mark are taste testing wings and she's got beer foam on her upper lip, it's utterly adorable, but it's the conversation they're having that is getting me.

"Seriously Mark, you gotta get out of your head. Text her and ask her on a date. She's obviously into you." She's licking sauce off her fingers and I'm trying not to pop a boner at how adorable she looks, especially with my hat on her head right now. "Girls don't invite guys to family events if they aren't interested!"

"Are you sure?" Mark straightens his posture a bit.

"Marky Mark, trust me. I've spent time with a bunch of women in my life, and in case you haven't noticed . . . I *am* a woman. If I didn't like Wyatt, I wouldn't have come to a hockey game with him and his friends." She raises an eyebrow at him before licking sauce off her fingers. I love seeing her walls down in front of my friends.

"You like Wyatt?" Austin gasps with fake shock.

We all chuckle and Whitney stares at me from across the table, smirking. "I did, but now I think I might leave with Frankie."

Frankie holds his hands up, innocently shaking his head.

I chuckle, patting Frankie on the back. "I don't think he'd be able to survive your sass, but you two feel free to try it out."

Whitney frowns and I realize my humor didn't translate. I don't want to embarrass her in front of the guys and apologize or reach out to her, but I see the look in her eye.

Fear.

Fear that I'd throw her to the side so easily, because that's what every man has done to her before me.

So, I pivot and say. "Would you like to come camping with us next weekend?"

She looks up at me with confusion. "What?"

I tap Frankie's foot, hoping he'll jump in and help save a potentially sinking ship.

"Yeah, we go for a hike and camp in the woods by a lake. It's a yearly tradition. It's a big group of us, it's super fun!" Frankie pipes in, nodding.

"It's us and our gals and two of our other friends, Dan and Evan. They're all super nice and have been dying to meet you," Mark adds in. "You've been nothing more than a mystery who Wyatt somehow woo'd."

"I am the Woo King, don't ya know," I joke, earning a laugh from everyone.

Mark eyes me and Whitney and then he leans into her and whispers something. She lets out a long breath and her eyes find mine. The light is back in her eyes.

"Count me in," she says quietly, her eyes turning to mine, as if she's trying to figure out if I actually want her there.

I see her shoulders relax when I meet her eyes, silently trying to convey that I want her to come.

"Do you know how to fish?" Mark asks her before I can speak up.

She nods slowly. "It's been a few years, but I can probably hold my own."

We settle back into a happy conversation, more beers and chicken wings and then we say goodbye to my friends.

As we walk towards my truck, I pull her against me. "I'm sorry, Whit."

"For what?" she whispers, but her shoulders tense and I know she knows what I'm referring to.

"For making you think I'd throw you away, if even for a moment. Because I wouldn't do that to you. I promise."

Her arm wraps around my waist tighter. "It's okay."

"No, it's not," I stop walking, turning to face her. "You're mine, okay?"

"Okay," she whispers.

"I mean it. Whitney; I need you to be mine." She looks up at me with her big green eyes and I search her face.

She tilts her face up to mine, kissing me.

"I already am, Wyatt." She pulls my hat off her head, moving it towards my head with a smile.

I hold my hand out for it, placing it back on her head. "No, you keep it. You wear my hat so well." I groan, pulling her back towards me.

I still feel bad for the joke I made earlier and the fear that had flickered in her eyes. She hasn't shown fear towards me since the first night at Scott's when I asked if she wanted a drink. I was surprised to see her drink alcohol tonight, even though it was just a beer. It took me a long time to be able to touch alcohol because of my dad. I always worried that if I had one drink too many that I would get angry like him.

Whitney's pinky grazes mine, bringing me back to reality. "Where did you go?"

"Oh. I was just thinking about how I was shocked that you drank tonight . . . not in a bad way . . . I just didn't expect it."

Whitney sits up in my bed, pulling her knees up to her chest, a wistful expression on her face. "It took me a long time to be okay with a drink or two . . . beer and wine is okay in moderation, and only in a place I feel safe in. Everything else is no go. Vodka especially." She explains, "Sometimes, growing up, my mom would give me alcohol. I was too young to understand, but I knew it tasted gross. She sent me to school smelling like booze more than a few times, but nobody seemed to notice or care. I was 'Trailer Trash Whitney' until April showed up, and even then, I was basically invisible to everyone but April and Scout."

I'm lost for words.

"Deacon and my mom are similar in the way they think every day should start with a strong drink. Sometimes Deacon would try to add stuff into my water . . . heck, he even tried to put vodka in my cereal one day."

I clench my jaw at her words, feeling anger rise in my chest. "That's fucked up."

"Yeah . . . anyway, one night after my mom's first radiation treatment, April and I bought a few kinds of alcohol—ones my mom didn't drink—and we did a taste test. It wasn't fun for either of us. The only thing we were okay with was Coors Light. I guess I wanted to see if I could drink with you, take another step forward in my healing journey . . . take that power back. And like most things, it feels easy with you."

"I can only drink beer too, and two is my maximum. I don't trust myself to try past that . . ." I blink up at the dark ceiling, my brain whispering: *I don't want to find out if I'm just like him.*

Her hand lands on my heart and as if she can read my mind she whispers, "You will never be *him*. You're a good man, Wyatt . . . No, a *great* man. *You* are perfect."

Chapter 23

WHITNEY

I love camping—anything that has to do with nature truthfully. April and I would camp out at her grandma's farm sometimes when my mom skipped town, or on the rare chance my mom would actually let me have a night away.

My favorite time to camp was during the fall when nights were cool, and stars were bright. Her grandma bought me a tent and a camping backpack for my thirteenth birthday, and I've always kept my gear at April's, afraid my mom would destroy it or try to sell it.

I meet Wyatt at his place, and he wraps me into a hug when he sees me. "There's my girl." He grabs my camping gear from me.

Earlier in the week Wyatt had given me a run down about who all was going and how long he's known all of them. He even gave me a few conversation pieces, as if he was trying to make sure I wasn't fully out of my element. He had also invited me to join Mark and him for dinner the other night because Mark wanted to tell me about how his date went.

"Are you excited?"

I chew on my fingernail. "Mostly. I'm still a bit nervous."

"I know this is a lot for you, and I'm really glad you decided to join me. I can't wait for you to meet more of my friends.

I'm in over my head . . . what if they hate me? What if I don't fit in?

"I know, Wy. I just don't want them to dislike me," I say, not meeting his eyes.

His finger grazes mine. "They'll love you, I promise."

I link my fingers in his, watching the road in front of us.

I really hope so.

Wyatt drives us towards the north side of Nashville, telling me about their camping trip last year and how it rained all weekend.

There are five other trucks on site when we arrive and the excitement on peoples' faces when they see Wyatt is like a punch to the gut. Only three people ever get excited to see me like that . . . Okay, maybe four. But it's clear everyone here has a soft spot for Wyatt.

I'll always be second choice to him won't I? Work and friends will always come first. This is a test . . . a test to see if we're a good fit.

Stop being cynical.

He's not Deacon.

Get out of your head.

Wyatt squeezes my hand before hoping out of the truck and I follow suit.

I'm grateful to see Frankie and Mark in the crowd of people coming over to greet Wyatt. But regardless, I stand on the other side of the truck, frozen.

Will he introduce me? Deacon never did, he'd forget all about me within seconds of seeing his friends.

Wyatt pulls back from hugging someone, scanning around until he sees me. He lets out a sigh before coming over to my side, pulling me into him. "Everybody, this is my girlfriend, Whitney!"

Girlfriend. Such a simple word but it fills my heart with a sense of security I didn't expect to feel.

I give a small wave to Wyatt's friend's, but they all do something that confuses me.

A chorus of, "It's so nice to finally meet you;" "He won't shut up about you;" "God, Wyatt she's so out of your league," ring through the group as they all move forward to hug me and greet me like they've known me forever.

I must look confused or mortified because Frankie whispers in my ear, "You are a part of his life, so you're part of *our* lives Whitney."

Wyatt plants a kiss on my forehead when introductions are complete. "I'll set the tent up. Do you want to help, or just hang out for a minute? I know this is a lot. I'm sorry, baby."

"I'm fine to get to know your friends, Wyatt." I motion my head towards a log where Frankie's girlfriend, Laura is sitting.

"You sure?"

"Positive. My therapist wants me to try feeling uncomfortable sometimes—test my anxiety in crowds. This is a good start, because you're here with me if I need a safety net."

Wyatt gives me a prideful expression, before kissing me. "You just keep getting stronger and stronger."

I move towards the log.

"Hey, Whitney," Laura greets me when I sit down beside her. She's gorgeous with dark curls and dark eyes, kind of similar to Paige.

I give her a genuine smile. "Hi."

"It's a bit overwhelming, isn't it? Six guys who are inseparable and three girls you've never met before. That was me last year. I ended up hyperventilating behind a bush." She lets out a laugh. "But they're such awesome people, especially Wyatt. He's kind of become like a big brother to me. That guy always has time to support anyone, especially the people he cares about."

I smile at her before turning to watch Wyatt, Frankie, and Mark pitching the tent. "He's definitely different from what I'm used to."

Once the guys have assembled the tent, they all turn to us with a "Ta-da" and exaggerated jazz hands.

Laura and I roll our eyes and laugh.

The group decides to set up a volleyball court and I opt just to watch. I might look like someone who would excel at volleyball, but it's not for me. My hand-eye coordination is better suited for baking and sewing.

My phone buzzes in my pocket as I watch the rest of them laughing. I pull it out of my pocket and answer, not looking at the caller ID—assuming it's April.

"Hello?"

"Whitney." Hearing my mother's voice for the first time in almost four months fills my throat with fills.

"Why are you calling me? How do you have my number?"

I changed it after the attack . . . Who would give it to her?

"It doesn't matter. I need money, Whitney." Her voice comes out jagged and I hear the clatter of bottles in the background.

"Mom, I can't do this right now."

"I owe Deacon money; doesn't that mean anything to you? Don't *I* mean anything to you?"

I try not to laugh at the irony—the question I asked her countless times in my life coming full circle.

I let out a big breath trying to keep my voice steady as I say, "That's not my issue," Pacing, I scan the shore line hoping there will be something I can fixate on.

"Come on, he threatened to sic his lackeys on me, like he's in the mafia and not just some low life junkie." Her tone shifts, annoyance easy to detect.

I know I should hang up and not give her the time of day, but anger rises to the surface before I can regroup. "I love how you say that as if you're not a junkie yourself. I can tell that you're high right now. I'm not an idiot." I pace further away from the campsite feeling my emotions starting to unravel.

Not this. Not right now.

I know that looking at Wyatt might calm me, but I don't want to risk crying in front of his friends.

"He said if you fuck him, he'll cut my debt in half," she says before taking a long drink, her gulps loud.

"You're disgusting. I'm done, Mom."

"Fuck you, Whitney. You are the most heartless person in the universe. Either fuck him or I'll get him to finish the job Carl couldn't." She hangs up before I can answer.

My knees give out as her voice trickles through my thoughts.

You *can't outrun this life, Whitney. You were born to be less than ordinary. You were born to be worthless.*

Chapter 24

WYATT

"Wyatt, I think something is wrong," Frankie states, pointing over to where Whitney is pacing, her entire body vibrating. I pass the ball to Dawson and sprint towards her just in time for her to fall onto the ground.

She's blinking back tears, trying to suppress them.

"Whit . . ." I cradle her against my chest. "What happened? Did something happen with April? Ellie?"

She shakes her head and her eyes gloss over and I see her put on a mask as she stands up. "Well, let's get back to the volleyball game, why don't we?"

Her voice sounds fake.

"Whitney." My voice comes out sharper than I mean it to, and her eyes widen.

She glances towards the water, before turning back to me. "Can we wait until later, please. I don't want to ruin today . . ."

I don't like that she doesn't want to tell me, but I'm also not about to make a scene in front of everyone if that's what Whitney wants.

"Can you just tell me who was on the phone?"

She closes her eyes and nods slowly. "We can talk about it later; I don't want your friends thinking I'm a bundle of emotions."

I feel a heavy protectiveness fill my chest as I say, "They wouldn't. Baby . . . don't shut me out, please. Don't put a wall up."

She lets out a long sigh, an apologetic expression crossing her face.

"It was my mom. But please, can we wait to discuss this later, after I email my caseworker and lawyer?" Her eyes are pleading, and my heart softens as she puts her hand on my chest.

I hesitate for a moment before saying, "Okay, but if something else happens today, you tell me, please."

"I will." Her voice is small. "I'll send the email now and then put my phone in the tent, so I don't have to worry about it."

"Do you want me to stay with you while you write it?" I offer, pulling her tight against me.

"Yes. Please," She whispers, a slight quiver in her lip as she opens a new draft for emails.

I sit quietly while she types it out and as soon as the email is sent, she notifies April and Ellie as well.

Whitney presses her head against my heart. "Thank you for sitting with me through that. I just want to move past everything—be done with that chapter of my life."

I know exactly how she feels, and I hope she can find that closure whether through whatever comes from her mom's trial, or finally having peace from her one way or another.

I grab her hand in mine and pray that the afternoon will be fun enough for her to truly get into her comfort zone again.

"Whitney, come sit!" Laura calls her over to the picnic table with the other girls.

I give her a firm kiss on the forehead and fight back the urge to say the words that consume the spaces of my heart.

I return to the volleyball game, trying to clear my mind, but I want to know what her mom said on the phone, and why she's trying to wiggle her way back into Whitney's life.

She's so good with my friends, and they all take to her like she's been part of the group forever. I appreciate how much everyone tries to involve her in the conversation and get to know her. She puts her head down when people ask about her family and where she grew up, but when I mention Scout and April, her light comes back to her, and she talks about her time on the farm.

"Wow, I've always wanted to live on a farm and have fields of crops," Mark says, earning a laugh from me.

"What?"

"Dude, you are the least country person I know, and you've killed every plant you've ever owned," I remind him.

He opens his mouth to protest before shaking his head. "Okay. I can't argue with that."

"And let's not forget all the goldfish he's murdered in his life," Austin chips in.

"I was seven, they looked skinny. I thought they were starving." He groans. "My mom shouldn't have trusted me."

A few people swap pet stories, but Whitney and I stay silent. I always wanted a dog growing up and she's mentioned a few times in passing that she would love a pet when she has her own place.

"Who wants to take a nature walk before starting dinner?" Frankie asks and we all agree to join him. Nothing beats the fresh November air.

Whitney walks with Frankie and Laura, leaving me to walk with Mark.

"Is she okay?" Mark asks quietly.

"Her mom is trying to cause issues, but I'm hoping it'll pass," I whisper, giving him a look of reassurance.

"Is she . . ." He doesn't finish his sentence, but I know exactly where his thoughts have gone. Mark is no stranger to abuse either; his sister got with a guy who did a number on her.

"Yeah, she's abusive. Between Whitney's home life and her ex-boyfriend . . . she's dealt with far more than I ever had to."

I shove my hands in my pocket, trying to push down my emotions.

"Don't do that. Don't diminish your childhood. Your dad was a monster, Wyatt. You came out of it a far better man than I ever would have been."

"I worry that I'll come face to face with her past and that everything I've worked for will be gone. I have so much anger towards them, what if I turn into my dad?" I admit.

Mark pats my back. "It's not the same thing and you know it. You want to protect her, not destroy her."

We come to a clearing and a smile spreads across my face as I look at the fields in front of us. It's a mix of tall grass and flowers growing despite the chill of winter coming soon.

I call out to Whitney, "Where are the wildflowers?"

She looks back at me, throwing her head back as she lets out a laugh. "They're right here, Wyatt."

Mark looks at me with confusion and I just smirk as I move towards her. "It's kind of our thing."

When I reach the field, I can't help myself. I pick her up and kiss her hard before I spin her around. Her arms circle my body, and a giggle escapes her lips when I pull back.

"Such a romantic fella, aren't you," she says, running a hand through my hair.

"Always," I reply before I start picking flowers.

Whitney moves right beside me, picking a bunch of orange and red ones.

She tilts her head towards the sky and whispers, "Hi, Scout."

I say a silent thank you to Scout, for sending literal wildflowers to Whitney. She looks so peaceful as she moves through the field, like every weight and burden she holds onto rolls off her shoulders.

I take my phone out of my pocket and snap a picture of her as she inhales the scent of the wildflowers. She opens her eyes, and we share a long look.

"Does anyone want to make me a flower crown?" Mark calls out, teasingly.

Whitney holds up her hand full of flowers. "Don't joke with me. I know how to make them."

My smile widens. "Make me one?"

"Of course, Wy."

"Me too!" Frankie shouts out.

Everyone else makes sounds of agreement.

"I'll do you all one better. I'll teach you all how to make one." Her expression makes my heart pinch. She looks so proud of herself as she clutches the flowers to her chest.

We all gather more flowers before heading back to the campground and over the next hour Whitney teaches us all how to make flower crowns with the utmost patience.

God, I love her.

We're sitting around the fire, all wearing our flower crowns with pride—some a little more lopsided or mangled than others. Mark is strumming his guitar as we all talk about our worst camping experiences, and Whitney contorts her face at some people's stories. But when people ask if she's got any stories, she tells them she's never been camping before.

I don't correct her, instead I turn the attention back on me. "Mark, you remember the year we went camping with your uncle and there was no running water and you got heat stroke?"

"Oh shit, yeah. That was not a fun time."

Whitney nods along as Mark tells everyone how we had to drive into town almost two hours away in order to buy water. Anyone would think that she's paying attention, but her eyes are glazed over slightly, and I don't miss the way she's chewing on her cheek.

When we get back to the tent at the end of the night she flops down on the air mattress with a long sigh.

"What's on your mind?" I ask when she places her head in her hands.

"I have a camping horror story."

"Do you want to share it, or would you rather not?" I crouch down in front of her, trying to read her tone.

"Yeah, but . . . It's kind of . . . dark," she says with an awkward laugh.

Whitney straightens her back and clears her throat.

"I was seven or eight, my mom and stepdad were drunk and high on all sorts of shit so I was in charge of keeping the fire maintained. But my stepdad fell into the tent and impaled his arm on the metal peg keeping it upright. Anyway . . . my mom laughed so hard she pissed herself and then when she lost consciousness, I had to find a park ranger to help us. We ended up spending the night in the hospital and Child Services was called."

"*Jesus,*" is all that my brain can muster.

Whitney purses her lips, letting out a long laugh. "Right? I still don't fully know why they let them take me home. That was the last time I went camping with them. I think that's why April and Scout worked so hard to create good camping experiences for me—even if it was just in the backyard during the daytime most of the time."

We swap some more positive camping stories and talk about our love of nature, curled up in each other while crickets and rustling leaves are our quiet soundtrack.

"Hey," she whispers against my neck. "I love your friends. I love seeing you all interact and lean on each other. It reminds me of what I have with April and Ellie."

I press my forehead to hers and bite my tongue. I'm falling for her fast and hard. It's not the kind of love I'll outgrow. Whitney Harris has pinned herself to my heart and I'm not going to let her walk away from me.

Whitney hugs me against her until a chill runs through our bodies. I give her one of my sweatshirts and then we both settle into the sleeping bag together.

She lies against me and tells me everything about her phone call with her mom and how she used to help pay off her mom's drug debt to Deacon with sex, how she didn't want to drag me into the drama. My heart hurts for her for carrying so much weight on her own, but I'm glad she trusts me enough to tell me.

The case worker arranges to meet with Whitney when we get back from the weekend, agreeing that it's probably safer for Whitney to be out of town for a few days.

If I need to spend every waking hour protecting her from them, I'll do it. I'm not going to let her mom or Deacon go anywhere near her.

We hold each other tightly, as if willing the monsters away.

"Wyatt . . ."

I turn to face her shadowy silhouette. "Yeah?"

"Thank you for letting me into your world, thank you for making me feel like your equal. Thank you for being the best man I've ever met. I . . . you're kind of one of my favorite people."

Her words fill my heart. "Whitney, my little wildflower, you are the best thing that has ever happened to me. You make me better than I was before."

Whitney sniffles and I hold her closer to my chest and kiss her gently at first, but then Whitney pulls me against her with a neediness I don't expect. She is urgent as she moves her body against mine, peeling our clothes off layer by layer until I am naked on top of her.

I dig into my bag to find a condom and put it on, entering her slowly. She clings to me as I move myself in and out. Small whimpers escape her lips as I hold her hips in place, letting our bodies melt together. I stare at her, searching into her soul as an orgasm rolls through her body. She covers her mouth to suppress her noises and I can't help but smile as we both explode together.

Chapter 25

WHITNEY

When I got in the house April was waiting for me, as was a cop and my lawyer. They had already drawn up a new restraining order against my mom, one that has more weight and can result in longer jail time for her getting too close to me. One is now in place for Deacon too. The cops went to do a wellness check on my mom, but told me that she wasn't at her house, and it looked like she hadn't been there for weeks.

I went to my therapy session after the meeting, grateful that I could share my feelings. The next few days I try to live my life as normal as possible, outside of having April and Wyatt on high alert, and driving me to and from work. Every night I toss and turn, trying to figure out my next move. And, every night, my eyes close and nightmares consume me, one after another.

I lazily roll over in bed, aware that April won't be sleeping beside me anymore, she's always been a morning person

My phone dings from the bedside table, stirring me and when I read the email my body goes cold.

Good morning Whitney,

Thank you again for your interest in subletting apartment 432 in the Valley View Building. Your application and reference checks have all been approved and your first and last month's rent has been deposited. Keys have been delivered to your current residence and signed for by Mrs. April Maren. Please contact us if something has changed.

Sarah Pratt, Broker

Berke Real Estate

576-555-1789 ext. 701

sarah.pratt@berkerealestate.com

Nashville, TN

What the hell?

I read and reread the email ten times.

They didn't . . .

"APRIL!!" I scream, jumping out of bed, flinging my door open like the house is on fire.

When I get to the kitchen, April and Ellie are sitting quietly, as if they've been waiting for this moment.

As if they expected me to react this way.

I grind my teeth together as I stare at the both of them. "Why?"

April goes to speak but Ellie holds her hand up. She rarely speaks over April, especially when I'm on edge so it catches me off guard. "Don't be mad, Whitney. This is your early Christmas gift from us. This is every birthday and milestone you didn't celebrate in your life—whatever answer will let you accept this."

April gives a slow nod, approaching me. "It's time you catch your footing, truly. A fresh start. You need this."

I collapse onto the couch, a swirl of emotions consuming me. My whole world is on display for everyone like a soap opera. "But my mom and Deacon . . ."

"The restraining order is in place no matter where you are. But it's worth noting that it's five minutes from work and five minutes from Wyatt's; ten Minutes from Grant and Bree's, and thirteen minutes from Paige's and sixteen minutes from here. We've mapped it out numerous times. There are cameras in the parking lot and hallways, and it requires a code to get into the building. It's secure."

"Why didn't you tell me you were doing this?" I scratch the side of my head, trying to figure out why they would hide this from me.

"It happened Friday after you and Wyatt left for the weekend. I'd inquired with the Berke's and they apparently had a move-in fall through, so it's move-in ready for you," Ellie tells me.

April nods eagerly from beside her, "We had planned to tell you when you got back, but then we had everything happen . . . Ellie got a good deal through the Berkes. You can afford it on your Elm Contracting wage without needing to pick up restaurant shifts anymore. We want you safe, but we also want you to move forward," April says, coming to sit on the coffee table in front of me. "It's time for the caterpillar to become a butterfly."

"Just look at it . . ." Ellie adds, quietly, pulling her phone out of her pocket. I scan through the photos and try to keep my excitement at bay. It really is a nice place.

I let out a long sigh. "You promise I can afford it . . . ?"

Ellie leans her head on my shoulder. "Yes, Whitney. I would never set you up for failure."

I look between my two best friends and smile. "Okay. I want it. I guess I gotta get packing."

I hug the both of them and then the three of us head to my room to pack my stuff up.

April twiddles her fingers. "Whitney . . . your other stuff?"

I meet her eyes, and something clicks in my head. "*Shit.*"

I never had an attachment to anything in my house, except for one item. And it's hidden under the floorboard beneath my rickety old bed. I don't know how I could have forgotten about it.

I meet April's eyes and whisper, "I have to get it."

"The cops said she hadn't been home for weeks so it shouldn't be a problem, right? I can come with you . . ." she offers but the flower crown on my dresser catches my eye.

Ellie and April follow my gaze and I let out a breath.

"He doesn't know that you're getting your place today, but he knows it's happening at some point. Scott and I let it slip yesterday. I wasn't expecting it to happen so fast. I know he'd come with you if you asked him to," Ellie says, reading my mind.

I close my eyes, an overwhelming need for Wyatt to know me deeper filling my gut.

April holds my phone out towards me. "It's your choice."

"He hasn't even met you properly yet . . ." I whisper.

She smiles. "Well today is as good a day as any. But right now, let's focus on getting your things back."

I nod before opening my text chat with Wyatt.

Whitney: Hey.

Wyatt: How's it going, gorgeous?

Whitney: Okay . . . I was hoping I could ask you a favor.

Wyatt: Anything.

I feel my heart tighten.

Whitney: Can you bring me to my mom's house? There's something I need to get.

Two seconds later my phone rings. It's him.

"When should I pick you up?"

"Whenever. And if you want to come with me to my new apartment, that's also cool."

"Wait, say that again?" he exclaims.

I smile at April and Ellie, as they watch me with glossy eyes. "My new apartment."

"Whitney, this is such a big day for you! I'll be there soon, okay?"

April and Ellie both hug me as soon as I hang up. "We're taking the day off. But we have to go and do something this morning first. I'll call your caseworker and ask her to go with you, as a precaution," April tells me. "We'll leave you be, I know you want time alone right now."

I sit on the side of the bed until the front door closes, my brain swirling with emotions.

Eventually I get up, put on my favorite purple jumpsuit and run a brush through my hair.

Trying not to pace, I move towards the front window, feeling my legs jitter. My only thought is that he'll run when he sees where I grew up.

His truck pulls into the driveway, so I throw my shoes on and head outside.

I lock the front door and take him in, he's singing along to the radio and his eyes are traveling up and down my body as I open the passenger door.

"Hi," I say quietly.

"Hey." He turns towards me. "I'm proud of you, and I want you to know how brave this is. Whatever you need from me . . . okay?"

I fold my hands in my lap and chew on my lip just as my case worker, Samantha, pulls up behind us in her cop car. I motion for her to follow us. I give Wyatt directions to my street, and his hands tighten on the steering wheel as we drive. He knows that neighborhood—everyone does. The majority of the crime statistics including drugs, assault, and more comes from my old neighborhood.

We don't speak to each other, but my brain is loud as we approach the cluster of trailers with broken windows, peeling paint, and overgrown front yards that all mirror each other.

Chapter 26

WHITNEY

When we get to my rundown house—if you can even call it that—I see that my mom's piece of junk car is in the driveway and my stomach drops.

Maybe she left it here.

"What do you need me to do?" Wyatt asks me, as he parks the truck.

I feel a lump grow in my throat, and I shake my head. "I don't know, honestly."

He takes the keys out of the ignition and says, "Together, it is."

Together.

Samantha gets out of her car, but I call out, "It should be okay."

I walk up our driveway cautiously, hoping Wyatt ignores the discarded beer cans, weeds, and cigarette butts scattered around, and by the time I reach the front door my hands are shaking.

I close my eyes as I turn the knob.

My mom is on the couch with a frown on her face as she rolls a joint with a half empty bottle of vodka beside her. "What the hell are you doing here? Did you bring my money?" Her eyes narrow as she looks over my shoulder, at Wyatt.

"I didn't think you'd be here. The cops said the house was empty," I mumble at the same time that Wyatt smiles at her, politely.

"You called the cops? Seriously? And who the fuck are you?" my mom snaps.

"My name is Wyatt. It's a pleasure to meet you, ma'am."

She doesn't acknowledge him, instead she looks over at me. "No guests. You owe me months of rent. Also, Deacon is looking for you." Her sinister smile says everything I need to know.

I exhale. "He's not a guest, and we're not staying." I make my way towards my room and Wyatt follows, stepping around the piles of dirty laundry on the floor.

I walk into my room and find everything ripped apart, my bags of clothing, my desk, my bed all flipped over.

It doesn't shock me.

"What the fuck are you doing?" she snaps at me, standing in the doorway to my room. I ignore her as I collect a few articles of clothing.

Instead, I turn to Wyatt and say, "Can you take some of the stuff out to the car? Let our friend know my mom is here." He looks at me, unsure and I give him a half smile before mouthing, "It's okay." He grabs as many bags as he can and jogs out of my room, as if it was a race for him to return.

My mom glares at me as she watches me move around my room. "Are you fucking moving out? You ungrateful child! Are you moving in with that man? You know how well it went last time."

"No, Mama, I'm moving out to live by myself. And in case you haven't noticed, I haven't lived here for almost five months now." I hold my gaze on her.

She lets out a loud snort. "Oh, just look at who finally grew a backbone, it only took you twenty-two years."

Laughing, I shift the mattress back onto the bed frame. "Twenty-four, actually. Nice to know you *still* don't know your daughter's age . . ."

She scoffs at me, moving towards me aggressively, "You'll last two days before you come crying back to me. You're weak and pathetic! I wish you were never born. You're nothing to no one you bit—" She raises her hand as she staggers towards me. I flinch, but before she can swing, Wyatt enters the room and grabs her arm.

"Touch her, and you'll be brought down to the station," he says firmly.

My mom gives out an evil laugh. "Yeah? Go ahead, they can't arrest me for having a fuck up of a daughter!"

Wyatt moves her backwards and comes to stand in front of me, to protect me. "Maybe not, but they can arrest you for possession of illegal drugs; they can deem your house unlivable with all the rot and black mold, and last I checked, threatening to kill someone won't help your track record. *Especially* while you're awaiting trial. If you'd like me to talk to the cop outside, I can bring her in," he says as he pulls out his cellphone.

My jaw hangs open as my mom grunts.

"She's worthless, anyways. She'll get what's coming to her one way or another. If you want to put up with her shit, all the power to you." My mom storms out of my room, swearing under her breath and I hear the clatter of vodka bottles from the kitchen.

Wyatt turns around to face me, worry filling his face. "Are you okay?"

I look down, trying to slow my breathing. "N-no, I just need to get . . . out of here."

He gives me a reassuring smile, picking up another pile of clothes. "At your service."

I bend down and pull out the floorboard, a wave of relief passing through me when I see the book come into view.

When Scout died, she left her copy of *To Kill a Mockingbird* for me, it includes notes on each page, and tucked underneath the book is a collection of notes she wrote to me over the years.

Wyatt is silent as he watches me, and when I stand up and take one last look around the room, I feel the weight of resentment and anger exit my body, "Let's go. There's nothing else I need here."

I feel no regret as I leave my room, suddenly glad that I'll never come back here, never have to deal with her abuse ever again.

As I'm walking out the front door my mom grabs my arm, she's got a joint in her hand. "You never come back here. You are dead to me."

A million thoughts run through my head but instead I gently remove her hand from my arm and say, "Goodbye, Karen." I don't turn around, but one single tear falls from my eyes as I follow Wyatt to the truck.

I think you're dead to me too, Mom.

After a short conversation with Samantha, we get into Wyatt's truck, while she goes to talk to my mom.

He backs out of the driveway and his hand finds mine, but he doesn't speak.

Instead, he drives us a few blocks away before stopping the truck.

"What?" I ask with confusion.

"I just need a second. Sorry." He's taking deep breaths as if he's trying to calm himself down.

I clutch the book to my chest as I stare out the window and sigh. "Wyatt, I appreciate you coming with me and I'm sorry I wasn't more transparent about my mom. I've never brought someone into *that* place before, not even April. I just want you to know that you break my walls down more than anyone I've ever known."

"Never ever apologize for protecting your heart . . . I'm just . . . seeing that house and seeing her raise a hand at you . . . it . . . *killed* me." His voice cracks, causing my heart to tighten.

"Hey. I'm okay, Wy. You kept me safe. You got me out of there in one piece."

He covers his eyes, as if he's trying to fight back tears. "I'll do anything to help you, Whitney. You are such a beautiful soul and I hope you can accept that you have people who are rooting for you."

My heart grows warm as his words roll through me. *Wyatt, my protector . . . my . . .*

"Are we dating?" I blurt out. "I mean you called me your girlfriend while we were camping, but you never fully asked me."

Wyatt lets out a long laugh. "Ah. I guess I didn't. Sorry, let's try again . . . Will you be my girlfriend? I only want you, baby, so be my whatever. Whatever you want, as long as it's you and me."

I take in his kind eyes, his smile, his stubble. He's everything I never thought I deserved. *He's everything.*

My eyes well up and my heart tightens.

"Hey, Whit . . . don't cry."

He cradles me against him and rubs my back.

And this man has the audacity to start singing "My Girl" by Dylan Scott to me. The song that reminds him of me. The one that reminds me of him.

My tears turn into laughter.

"My singing isn't that bad!" He chuckles alongside me.

I can't help myself, I grab him and kiss him, hard. I hope it screams thank you in a million different ways. He pulls back from me with a goofy grin. "I assume that meant thank you . . ."

I nod, licking my lips. "Yeah."

"Well, you are very welcome . . . Anyway, on to our next stop!"

"My apartment?" I try to hide the smile in my voice.

"No, April reached out to me saying we're to meet her somewhere else first." He puts his truck into drive, giving me a sad smile, "Whitney." His tone is soft. "I . . . I can't believe she's your mother. I've never felt so angry on someone else's behalf. I'll never let anyone hurt you again. I promise. Nobody will ever break you. Scout's honor."

I laugh. "Like my Scout or Boy Scout?"

"Both. Always both."

I give him a long smile, picturing Scout up in heaven kicking her feet in glee at me finding someone who treats me so well.

Someone who makes me feel whole.

I glance in Wyatt's direction, watching him intently and without warning my heart explodes in the most subtle way possible.

Holy fuck.

I love him.

Chapter 27

WYATT

Whitney is quiet as we drive. I know today has been a lot for her to handle, but I also know that seeing her apartment will turn it around for her. I think she will be happy to find out what we have planned for her.

I pull into the parking lot of Moe's Mattress Land, and we head towards the store. There's no way I'm letting her sleep on the floor tonight.

"Ah. I guess a bed is a good start." She lets out an awkward laugh as we head into the store.

"I'd say so."

We move around a few mattresses, and I see Whitney checking the price tags of every mattress she touches, her anxiety rising with each one she passes. She tries to move towards the single beds and I'm about to tell her not to when April steps through the front door. When she reaches us, the two of them hug each other tightly. I watch the two of them talk and cry. The depth of their bond is evident from the ease with which they interact.

But suddenly April looks over at me with wet eyes and she giggles out a, "Fuck yes, bestie," and then she comes towards me and hugs me something fierce.

"Thank you," she says with fresh tears. Poor Moe must think we've lost our minds.

"Hi, April. Nice to see you again."

April turns towards Whitney, who is walking towards us cautiously, and says, "Go away, go over there."

With a lopsided grin, Whitney chuckles and follows her direction.

April turns back to me, and I can tell she's sizing me up.

"Thank you for going with her. I don't want to know what it was like, because I know I'll beat myself up more than I already do. I know you understand she doesn't let people in easily, but I've known her most of my life and I've never seen her like this before. You bring something out in her. But as her sister I have to say this . . . hurt her and I will end you. I am not making the same mistake again." She's smiling as she says it, but I know she means it.

"I'll try not to hurt her, April. I'm so proud of her right now and I get why she's so caring and why she powered through all these years. It's you, and your grandma. You were her first family, and I will never try to replace you.

"You're a good guy Wyatt. She's lucky. You're lucky too."

Like I needed a reminder of how lucky I am?

We both laugh before April claps her hands together. "Alrighty then. Let's go buy our girl a mattress."

Whitney is adorable at the best of times but she's all the more adorable when she rotates between making April or I lie beside her.

April rolls her eyes and tells Whitney to get something she likes so she finds the firmest mattress. One with a bit of memory foam and April and I exchange a sad look. I don't doubt that April knows how minimal Whitney's mattress was. I barely glanced at it when I was in her room, and I was able to tell that it was barely two inches in depth.

She deserves this.

I motion to Moe that we want this one and fifteen minutes later I wrangle it into the back of my truck.

April meets us at the apartment but it's Ellie leaning on the wall that shocks Whitney.

"What are you doing here?" She looks between Ellie, April and I, trying to make sense of what is happening.

"Just checking in . . ." Ellie says, pulling her into a long hug. Whitney stares between the three of us but says nothing. "Anyway, you and April are going out for a while until I text her. No questions asked."

Whitney nods slowly, confusion written across her face.

"Chop, chop!" Ellie puts her hands on her hips, and I chuckle.

"Okay, geez. I'm going, Miss Bossy-pants," Whitney replies, playfully.

Ellie pulls her into a hug again and whispers to her and then the two of them are crying.

I may have just seen the woman who broke her, but now I'm watching the women who helped heal her and it's one of the most refreshing things to witness.

"Okay, now shoo! Go have fun." Ellie laughs, waving her away.

Whitney hugs her again before turning towards me. "I don't know what you're up to, Wyatt Morgan . . . but if you make me cry any more today, I may turn into a pile of dirt."

I pull her against me. "I'll bring the broom and dustpan, baby." I kiss her hard and give her one last squeeze before April whisks Whitney away.

I turn to Ellie and smile. "Ready?"

"Damn straight. It's showtime!" she exclaims before leading me into the building where the others are already waiting for us with cans of paint and sheets scattered around the space, making a good headway on everything.

"Alright, where do we start?" I clap my hands together.

"You can do the second coat in her bedroom," Scott calls out to me as he paints the living room wall.

I head into the master bedroom and it's three times the size of the room she grew up in. I swallow the lump in my throat and get to work.

Ellie, Scott, Paige, and I spend the next three hours working our magic.

Painting, placing furniture, filling the fridge, hanging photos on the wall.

Giving Whitney a home.

When we finish, Scott shakes his head, taking in the finished space. "You really like her, huh?"

I nod, looking down. "Yup, I really fucking do."

More than that.

Ellie leans against the counter. "This is the sweetest thing I've ever witnessed in my life, Wyatt. I knew you were one of the good ones, but I don't know too many guys who'd do this."

"Hey, I'd do this for you!" Scott throws in.

Ellie laughs, patting his arm. "When I was twenty-four? I don't think sooo. Pretty sure you were too busy stealing my dream house from me."

She gives Scott a pointed look and Paige and I snort.

My phone buzzes. "April got my text. They're on their way back now."

Paige claps her hands together. "Here goes nothing!"

Chapter 28

WHITNEY

April takes me to lunch and refuses to talk about what the heck is happening at my apartment. It doesn't take a rocket scientist to know what Ellie Elm could be doing in an empty apartment—one that might need a fresh coat of paint or home-y touches.

Instead, she talks to me about any other topic—even resorting to the weather for a brief period. She wears her best poker face so eventually I stop trying to force things out of her and order myself a giant piece of chocolate cake.

"So, gatekeeper, when can I see what havoc they've been causing in my new place?" I try to give her my best, innocent doe eyes, hoping she'll crack and tell me what she knows.

"Whenever Ellie tells me to come back. I am a brick wall, Whitney Harris! You can stop trying to get information." She gives me a pointed look.

I groan but take a bite into my cake. "Fine. You win this round."

April grabs her fork, digging into my slice of cake. "Nah, Whit. We all win."

After three hours of anxious energy, she finally tells me to get into the car.

When we pull into the parking lot, Wyatt is leaning against the wall with a smile full of secrets.

"Have a nice girl date? What did you ladies do?" he asks as we approach. April nods but I just roll my eyes, wanting to skip the small talk.

"Better question is what have *you* been up to? Hmm?"

April laughs, linking her arm through mine as Wyatt opens the door for us both.

"Winning the best boyfriend award, hopefully." He smirks.

As we get into the elevator together, Wyatt watches the connection between April and I. I give him a reassuring smile, so he doesn't feel like the third wheel.

As we get out of the elevator, April lets go of my arm, ushering me forward. Wyatt holds back too.

"It's unlocked," he says quietly, motioning for me to move forward.

I open the front door and tears start to escape before my mind can process what I'm looking at.

The kitchen and living room are fully furnished with dark walnut accents and light purples and beiges. Wildflowers are in a vase on the kitchen table and cozy pillows and throw blankets cover the couch—including my grilled cheese blanket. A big screen TV sits on a stand and above it a sign that says Family, surrounded by pictures of April and I, group shots of the girls, and even a few that feature Scout.

The lump in my throat is overwhelming as I step further into the apartment and stare into the primary bedroom. The mattress is on a bed frame covered by a floral duvet. Beside my bed is a long purple dresser that has decor that screams Whitney. I feel my legs give out, and land on the floor on top of a plush light gray rug. Sobs rack through my body as I run my fingers through the material.

I can't believe this.

This is my home.

This is mine.

A few seconds later April is snuggling up behind me.

I sob harder. "You stole my vision board . . ."

"Come on, Whit. How many "dream homes" did we draw up over the years? Designing this place for you was easy as pie." April lets out a laugh. "But you're okay with everything?"

Am I okay with everything?

"April, you could have painted every room black, and I'd still love this . . . but . . ."

"No buts. You needed this, you deserved this. Don't fight, don't ask questions. Whitney, this is what your mom should have given you." Her voice catches and we cry some more. "I love you. Whit . . . and I'm pretty sure someone else might love you too."

We hug each other.

"Jesus, I've seen you cry like six times woman, where is this all coming from?" April teases, pulling me in against her. "But seriously, what do you feel like doing tonight? I know today has been hectic so if you want alone time, or just me, or just Wyatt . . . whatever you choose, we'll all support you."

As overwhelming as this day has been, spending the evening with the people who did this for me sounds like exactly what I need. "I best invite people over, to thank them for their hard work today."

"Are you sure you're up for that?"

"April, I want to be surrounded by *my* family tonight. To celebrate this new chapter of my life with people who have loved and supported me every step of the way."

She nods. "Okay, if that's what you want to do, then that's what we'll do. I like that idea."

I eventually sit up and wipe my eyes, leaning my head against her shoulder. "Sisters forever."

"Sisters forever," she echoes.

I turn to look at her and she reads my eyes crystal clear—a million *thank you's* cross between us silently. She gives my hand a hard squeeze. "I'll give you and Wyatt some time alone and let you process the day, but I can ask Ellie to invite everyone this evening, if you want me to?"

"Sure, that works. Send it to the group chat."

"Will do!"

She stands up and gives me one quick wave before I hear her and Wyatt exchange pleasantries. I lay back down on the rug and exhale.

A few seconds later Wyatt settles on the ground behind me.

"Hi." His voice sounds small.

Far away.

"Hi," I echo, rubbing my hands through the rug again.

"Have you even sat on the bed yet? Pretty sure it's more comfortable than the floor," he say with a hint of sarcasm.

I blink back fresh tears. "Why?"

"Beds are comfier than floors for many reasons . . . more cushioning . . . blankets?" Wyatt starts with a teasing tone.

I laugh, smacking his chest playfully. "No . . . like why. Why me? Why this? *Why*?"

His hand tilts my head up to face him. "Because you deserve the world. Whit, this is like one billionth of what you're owed. And before you freak out about us spending too much money on furniture, Ellie and Scott pulled stock from previous years' staging inventory. It's stuff that was collecting dust."

"So how much do I owe you for the mattress?" I bite my lip.

He rolls his eyes before replying. "You owe me nothing. Your happiness and safety is more than enough." He kisses my nose and I laugh as I pull him against me. "Whitney, my wildflower . . . I can't imagine my life without you."

We kiss for a long time before he pulls back with a frown.

"What?"

"I have to run out for a bit, go get changed, and pick some things up for tonight. I think you deserve some time to be in your space alone too, to process everything."

I nod. I should probably shower before everyone comes back, I'm a snotty mess.

"Thank you for this," I say to him. "Seriously, Wyatt. Nobody has ever done something so . . . grand for me."

"Baby, this is the least we can do."

As soon as Wyatt leaves, I open every cabinet, cupboard, closet, and touch everything. I even jump on my bed and squeal loudly, an overwhelming sense of freedom filling me.

After a long refreshing shower, in my own bathroom, I slip into a long sundress covered in wildflowers and I add a bit of curl to my hair.

A knock on the door sounds and I half expect Wyatt, but Ellie and Scott are there beaming at me. Should have known Ellie, the early bird, would be here first.

I pull her in for a hug and whisper, "Don't make me cry again. But thank you a million times for this."

Ellie squeezes me. "But I love making you cry, it's like my fifth favorite hobby," she teases before adding, "I love you, Whitney."

I pull back and smile at Scott.

"Are you a hugger now?" I ask him.

"Now?" He chuckles and pulls me in for a hug. "I was always a hugger, Whitney."

Wyatt appears in the doorway and sighs. "You two beat me."

He's changed into a denim button up and black jeans with a gift bag in one hand and a duffle bag in the other.

My heart explodes as I take him in.

His eyes scan me. "Fuck, you're gorgeous."

Scott snorts and I hear the sound of what I can only assume is Ellie smacking his chest.

Wyatt averts his eyes from Scott as I pull myself into him.

Ellie squeals. "Wait! Stay there. Smile." She pulls her phone out and snaps a picture of the two of us. "You look incredible together." And then she smacks Scott on the back of his head again. "And you'll forever be an ass."

"I love you too, Elenor." He ruffles her hair with a wink.

Everyone starts to arrive, and I realize I didn't prepare snacks or food. "Shit, y'all. I didn't make snacks."

April snorts and says, "Babes, did you open your fridge?"

"Uh. No . . ."

It's probably the one thing I didn't touch.

I open it and sure enough it's fully stocked with drinks and a few platters of already sliced fruits and veggies sitting beside a meat tray. I just laugh as I start unloading stuff onto the counters.

These people.

"Y'all are too much," I say, trying to blink tears away again. Thank goodness I didn't put mascara on today or I might have turned into a raccoon by now.

We gather around my dining room table and settle into playing board games—like sitting in this apartment is the most natural thing ever, instead of it being the first time we're all here.

Throughout the night, everybody shares about how excited they are for me and gushes over how nice this place turned out.

I've never felt so loved in my entire life.

At the end of the night, Wyatt wraps me into his arms after slow, emotional sex in my bed. My bed that doesn't sag. My bed that is warm and safe. My bed that isn't a temporary space.

My home.

"Wyatt . . ." I whisper into the darkness.

"Yes, Whit?"

"I don't remember the last time I slept with my bedroom door open."

Wyatt lands a kiss on my shoulder. "And now you'll be able to for the rest of your life."

Chapter 29

WYATT

I wake up alone in Whitney's bed and part of me panics—thinking this was all too much for her so she snuck back to April's house, but then I hear the sound of drawers opening and the gentle hum of the radio and my body relaxes.

I hop out of bed and creep towards the doorway. She's wearing leggings and a blue T-shirt tied at her waist, her hips moving with the rhythm of the music.

I never knew how such a simple moment of having someone dance around in a kitchen could make my knees weak, but it does. I know this adjustment might not be linear for her, but it's incredible seeing her so at home in this place already.

How at home I feel in this place . . . and with her.

It's like she took a sledgehammer to my heart and built me up brand new.

"Morning, sleepy head." She glances over her shoulder when she notices me. "Pancakes and bacon work for you?"

I walk towards her slowly. "That works for me. What can I do to help?"

"Tell me where I might find a pan?"

"Oh. I never gave you your gift!" I say, eyeing the bag on the counter.

Grabbing the bag, I extend it towards her. She digs into the bag and smiles as she pulls out a purple frying pan. "Well, thank goodness we have something to make the pancakes in now!"

She reaches into the bag again, laughing when she pulls out a loaf of bread.

"This is for all the grilled cheeses I'll make you," I say, sheepishly before she pulls out a recipe card holder.

She pulls the first few cards out and her eyes well up as she reads through the cards "Scout's Cinnamon Pancakes, Wyatt's Grilled Cheese Extraordinaire . . . Wildflower Waffles?"

I give her a coy smile, loving how excited she looks.

"Wy, this is so thoughtful. I love it so much!" She embraces me in a long hug before turning towards the stove. "Now, let's put this first recipe to use."

She pulls an apron over her head, looking absolutely adorable.

"I'm going to need an apron too."

"I can make you one on my next sewing day with April," she offers.

"I'd love that . . ." I reply, kissing her forehead. "Can you please make it say 'Kiss the Chef'?"

"That's so cliché, ya dork." Whitney giggles. "Maybe we can go look at fabric for it today? And go riding!" She beams. "Oh, wait no, you work. I work too!" she says, realizing it's a weekday. "We better get a move on . . ."

I kiss her temple before shaking my head. "Nah, our bosses decided they didn't want us around today."

She lets out a laugh. "Okay."

We cook together, side by side, and my heart keeps screaming out to tell her how I feel. To say the words. But the last twenty-four hours have been hectic enough for her, so many changes and things out of her control. I don't want to overwhelm her more.

"Where did you go?" Her voice breaks through my thoughts, and I turn to see her observing me in full.

"I, uh . . . was just thinking about how much I love . . . cooking with you," I say awkwardly before adding. "And how much I'm missing Jeff."

She nods, putting her head on my chest. "Well, thank goodness we're going riding today then!"

I shake drywall dust out of my hair as I get into my truck, knowing that my mom is going to call me soon. It's the first night in almost a week that I won't be staying at Whitney's place, and I feel on edge leaving her alone, even though I know April, Ellie, Bree, and Paige are there. After a few days of watching Whitney live in her own space, emotions have come to the surface for me–ones I can't place until my mom's name flashes across my screen.

"Hi, honey. How was work today?" Her tone is chipper but all I can hear is the words Whitney's mom said to her, and the way I watched the girl I love almost get hit.

"How did you walk around being okay with me covered in bruises? How did you let me stay in that house? Why didn't you leave him? Why did you let him hurt us?"

My voice is not my own as words spill out of me, I've never spoken to my mom like this.

"Wyatt . . ." She's sniffling, caught off guard by my tone.

"Fuck, Mom, I'm sorry. I met Whitney's mom and she's having to adjust to living on her own, and I guess I'm reliving what it felt like when I moved out . . . I just feel so out of body right now." I hang my head in my hands.

My mom is silent on the other end of the line for a long time, aside from her breathing.

"I tried to leave, Wyatt; many times . . . The first time you were six and your dad threw you down the stairs, the second time you were eight and you ended up with a broken wrist and the third . . . The third time he threatened to take you and your brother and drive you off a cliff and it was the first time he hit your brother—a warning to me. They were all warnings of what he would do if I left . . ."

Anger fills my chest as I think back to my childhood.

My mom continues to speak. "It was a blessing that your brother had a heart condition . . . that's fucked up." I've never heard her swear in my entire life, not even when my dad was hurting her. "Sorry. Clearly, we're both a bit riled up."

"What do I do, Mom?" I wrap my hands tightly around my steering wheel, blinking back unshed tears. "How do I make sure I'm brave for her while she starts another new chapter of her healing, without dumping everything on her. I don't want to add more stress or pain to her right now."

"Wyatt, I owe you a million things. I failed you—I'll never stop apologizing for that. I know what you are feeling right now is hard and scary. It's reminding you of all those years you tried to get Wesley and I out, but you need to remember, you are safe. *She* is safe."

Guilt fills my chest, my mom did the best she could with the cards she was dealt, I know that. But it's hard to sit here and remember what he did to her.

To us.

"Wyatt, you kept me from breaking so many times, you know that? Even from a young age, you were a calming presence. You still are. You were made to be a protector. You protected me, you've protected her, and you made your brother into the man he is today. You should be so proud of yourself for everything you've done, honey."

I let out a long sigh. "Mom, I love you. I'm sorry I blew up on you."

"You didn't . . . you just finally found your voice. You should have been yelling all this at me when you were fifteen. You're just too nice." She pushes out a deep breath. "She's strong and she has you, so she'll be okay."

"Seriously, I'm sorry for yelling, mom. That was out of line. I shouldn't take this out on you." I rub my eyes, still burning, still no tears.

"It's okay, It only took you twenty-seven years!" She lets out a laugh. "You were always too good. Yelling doesn't make you like him; you know that, right?"

"I know you always tell me that, but it's hard to separate."

"I get that. You were the best kid, Wyatt, and I was the worst mom." She whimpers.

"Trust me, Mom, you're not even close to the worst. You were just stuck in a bad spot."

We all were.

Chapter 30

WHITNEY

It's been almost two weeks since I moved into the apartment. My time has been filled with girls' nights, dinner dates with Wyatt, knitting in front of the TV, and doing whatever my heart desires. But most importantly, I've been sleeping soundly. My first few nights alone were strange, but I've come to enjoy the peace and quiet.

I love having my own space and how I don't feel like I need to tiptoe around on nights I get home late. If I make a mess, I can leave it for a few days without being yelled at or feeling guilty, and my place doesn't smell like years of mold and stale cigarettes.

Having my own place makes me feel like I've healed another part of myself. It makes me feel like I've moved forward all the more.

Being able to reread Scout's copy of *To Kill A Mockingbird* with all her little notes and scribbles means everything to me, and reading through her letters of encouragement and love are all the boost I need to keep moving forward.

I'm still a bit worried about Deacon or my mom showing up and trying to get a rise out of me, or hurting me, but knowing I'm safe in my apartment and that my friends are close brings me ease. I've spent the afternoon reading the book and when I turn the page, a folded piece of paper falls out.

I unfold it and instantly my heart sinks. My handwriting stares back at me, messier and younger, but when I see the first words, I remember the day vividly.

> *Dear Diary,*
>
> *I don't know if I can stay here anymore . . . at home or on earth. My mom hates me and I hate me too. I am so stupid and unimportant. My mom said I should just leave, live somewhere else. She doesn't want me anymore. I can't talk to her about anything, because everything I say is wrong. I don't know what to do anymore. But what scares me the most is that I don't think my mom would care if I'd die for her. I'll never be good enough for her.*
> *W.H.*

I wipe a few tears away, hating that even at a young age my mom held that kind of power over me. But as I read the words over again, I realize how much I have to be grateful for in life now, and how, despite the hell she put me through, I'm a stronger person than I could have ever imagined. I check the time on my phone, realizing that I have to head out to therapy soon. Grabbing my diary entry and a note from Scout, I know exactly what today's session will be about.

Dr. Boate listens intently as I read her the diary entry, before leading into the first note Scout ever wrote to me.

"Whitney, happy birthday, darling. I hope this next year of your life is filled with love, laughter, and as many pancakes as you want. You will always have a home here with April and I. You are our family, and we are yours. Love, Scout."

I fold the note in half before looking at Dr. Boate.

"How does reading both of those make you feel?"

I meet her eyes as I talk. "Like night and day . . . I spent so much time trying to find the reason why my mom could treat me like I was nothing and how someone who wasn't even related to me was able to make me feel more valued than my own mother. I guess what I'm continuing to realize is that I spent my entire life trying to find the good in her . . . give her the benefit of the doubt. But there were so many times I tried to turn to her, to give her the chance to help me through things. With April, Wyatt, and everybody else who is supporting me without expecting anything in return, I'm realizing that just because someone is blood, doesn't mean they are family." I let out a long sigh, fidgeting with the pillow on the couch beside me.

"Well, Whitney—because your mom will never tell you this—I'm proud of you, and you should be so proud of yourself, too. You're doing amazing and the growth I've seen from you in each session is incredible."

For the first time in my life, I'm able to say, "I'm proud of myself too," and the warmth that spreads through my chest lets me know that no matter where my life goes, no matter what comes next . . . I'm going to be okay.

I don't visit Wyatt at work often because I spend most days in the office, but I love watching him with his hat on backwards, lifting lumber like it's nothing more than a bag of skittles. Ellie asked me to come by the property today, although I have no idea why. So I make the walk towards the property after the camera crews are gone.

I see Grant and Mal sitting out on the front porch, drinking coffee in their T-shirts, unphased by the slight chill of the early December air. They both give a little wave as I approach.

Grant nods his head sideways. "Hey, Whitney. They're inside waiting for you."

I laugh as I reach them. "You make it sound like I'm in trouble."

"You just might be," he teases before giving me a quick hug.

I give Mal a hug too before heading inside.

Ellie and Scott are sitting at the kitchen table giggling together with paperwork in front of them and I stop in my tracks. "Uh . . . Hi?"

"Whit!" Ellie gets up and comes to hug me. "Thanks for coming. Please sit."

Scott gives me a salute. We get along really well. Maybe it's because we're both too stubborn for our own good, or because we're both dating the two sweetest humans in the world, but either way, I'll be team Scott for the rest of my life.

I sit down across from them, and they give each other a private smile. I can't help but love seeing her so happy. Ellie clears her throat and looks back at me with flushed cheeks.

"So . . ." she says slowly, her voice unreadable.

"Okay, can I just say you guys are making me *reaalllly* nervous . . . Am I fired already?"

Scott chuckles, eyeing Ellie. "I told you this would stress her out!" He looks back at me and pushes a document towards me. I pick it up in my hand and squint as I scan the words.

"I don't understand . . ." I look up at them both with confusion.

"We're making Elm Woods Contracting and Design official and we want *you* to be our Administrative Office Manager. You'd oversee the receptionists, our assistants, any staffing concerns . . . make sure Scott doesn't steal all my pens . . . that kind of stuff," Ellie tells me. Scott smirks as he twiddles an Elm Contracting and Design pen between his fingers.

I shake my head from side to side, staring at the hefty pay increase listed. "I . . . I don't know what to say. What about Scott's Office Manager? Shouldn't you hire someone with more experience instead?"

Ellie gives me a sad smile. "No, Whit. We want you. You've earned this."

"Besides, Jesse has been asking to lessen her hours, so it's actually doing everyone a favor," Scott adds.

"Did Wyatt make you do this?" I clench my teeth together, my face turning red.

Ellie senses my shift. "No, Whitney. This is on me and me alone. But Scott agrees fully with this move. Please don't think this is a handout. Because it's not." Ellie's eyes go wide as she speaks.

I scan the page, trying to ignore the line that mentions pay—an amount I never expected to make. It's more than twice what Ellie is currently paying me. "You promise this is not just a pity job? I don't want to let you down . . ."

Scott shakes his head. "We promise. We're both overwhelmed right now. We have so much going on with the show and all our other houses. Teaming up might seem silly to add to the list, but we figure it's better now than later. We need someone we can trust, someone who knows the ropes. I'll even let you borrow one of my nice pens," Scott adds with a wink.

"You mean *my* pens." Ellie laughs, swatting his shoulder.

"Potato, pota-toh baby girl," he says to her with a low chuckle and Ellie flushes.

"You guys are so mushy. You get that, right?" I raise an eyebrow at them.

"Hey, I think you and 'Wy' can be a bit mushy too," Scott challenges.

I purse my lips. "Elenor, control your man."

Ellie breaks into an infectious laugh. "God, I love you." She smirks at me, before turning towards Scott. "Told you she wouldn't take your shit either." She leans her head against his shoulder.

Scott laughs. "I know . . . I didn't believe you. I already have you and Paige who don't take my shit. I'm regretting this choice."

"Hey!" Ellie and I shout in unison, making us all laugh again.

"When will the official merge happen?"

Ellie gives me a secretive smile. "We'll be telling the crew when we have our watch party for the show next Friday, but we just secured an office space so we're working on the design choices now. We figured you should know first because you'll be getting to know more of Scott's team, and working at aligning our company policies and safety regulations," Ellie tells me.

"We know it's a lot . . . and it's fast, but we want you to have the time and space to look over things.

"Yeah, okay that wo—" I start.

"Whitney!" Wyatt's voice fills the room with so much joy that a blush creeps across my face. "Hey! What are you doing here?"

I turn towards him and smile. He's in dark jeans and a green T-shirt, sawdust covering his boots and his hard hat in his hand, looking utterly handsome.

He looks unsure how to greet me.

"Kiss her, Wyatt. We won't fire you for kissing your girl." Scott leans back in his chair with a smug smile. One that says, *I kiss my girl at work all the time*.

I hear Wyatt chuckle as he walks towards me. He kisses me quickly before catching sight of the contract in my hand.

He whips around to look at Ellie and Scott, excitement in his voice. "I knew it."

Scott smirks. "Yeah, well now you gotta keep it a secret for two weeks, okay?"

"I can handle that, we all know she would have run home to tell me anyway," Wyatt says, wrapping his arms around my shoulder.

He's not wrong . . .

"Oh hush." I giggle as Scott and Ellie smirk at us.

"Now give me the pen," I say, unable to hide my excitement.

Scott slides Ellie's pen across the table to me and I sign.

"Okay back to work for us," Ellie says, standing up. "You get five minutes, Wyatt, and then you're back to it. We need to get the bathroom done today," Ellie tells him before pulling Scott out of his chair.

"Welcome to my team too, Whitney!" Scott exclaims before they step past me, towards the living room.

"Our team!" Ellie corrects him with an eyeroll.

"Hey, Scott . . ." I call out, making them both turn back to face me. "First order of business, stop stealing Ellie's pen. I might have to write you up to HR." I wink at Ellie and Scott snorts.

"This is going to be fun," Ellie throws over her shoulder before they move to the next room. "I'll send you an email in a bit with some more information, okay? And I'll stop by the office this afternoon?"

"Sounds good!" I nod.

Wyatt pulls me into a hug once I stand. "I'd offer to show you the house, but it's a bit of a war zone aside from this room and I've got a lot to do today." He gives me an apologetic shrug.

"Wy, it's fine. I'm sure I'll have my hands full with the merger." I laugh.

"I'll walk you out," he offers as we move.

"Are you okay if I'm working in the same environment as you? I didn't even think about that. If you're uncomfortable I can tell them no and look elsewhere . . .you were on the team first so I would never expect you to leave." I look up at him, trying to read his face.

"Of course, yes . . . sorry . . . my brain is distracted today. I am so happy for you. You deserve this!"

"Thanks."

"Hey, want to come somewhere with me this weekend?" He sounds off but I try not to read into it too much, knowing that he's got to get back to work.

"Sure . . . where?" I offer my best innocent face, hoping it'll convince him to tell me.

He chuckles. "Good try, wildflower. It's a secret . . . Anyway, I should get back to work . . . I'll text you later, okay?"

"Sounds good."

We stand on the sidewalk staring at each other in silence before he pulls me in for a hug.

I find his heartbeat and sigh.

"Are you okay?" he whispers, unknowing of the fact his heartbeat recharges me.

"Yeah, I'm good." Never been better.

I can't hide the smile that crosses my lips as realization hits me . . . Wyatt is home to me.

Chapter 31

WYATT

I watch Whitney move down the sidewalk for a moment before heading back inside to finish tiling the shower wall. I'm so proud of her for accepting the job, though I'm sure she gave Ellie and Scott some grief for choosing her over our current Administration Manager at Woods Contracting.

I'm sitting in the shower, humming under my breath when Ellie and Scott come into the room.

"You have a minute?" Ellie asks me as they close the door behind them.

"Y'all wanna get cozy in here with me?" I tease them, readjusting myself so I'm facing them.

They chuckle in response.

"Maybe later." Scott smirks, earning a smack from Ellie.

"So, what's up?" I ask, taking in their serious facial expressions. I stand up. "I'm not in trouble for kissing my girl, am I?" I tease, earning a laugh from Scott.

"Oh, shut up man."

Ellie pulls out a stack of papers from behind her back and hands them to me. My initial thought is that it's some sort of form disclosing my relationship. But then my eyes land on the words: *Job title, Project Manager.*

"What do you think about overseeing some properties on your own?" Scott gives me a wide grin.

I stare between them and the contract in confusion.

Ellie steps towards me. "In the time since I've started working with you, I've taken notice of your great leadership and kindness, but more so in the last few months. I've watched you go from one stressful situation to the next without it interfering with your job . . . Scott and I have had countless talks about you, and ultimately, we think that you've earned a promotion."

I stare down at the page again and my eyebrows furrow as I read: *Project Managers, Wyatt Morgan and Grant Thompson, will be allotted office space D.*

"Are you telling me Grant and I are a team?" I try to hide my smile.

Scott laughs. "Yes, you two are like the new and improved Property Brothers, we couldn't separate you guys. Anyways, we'll give you some time to look over it."

I read over the contract slowly, laughing at the irony of me panicking, the way Whitney probably had barely an hour ago.

This is something Scott and I talked about years ago, but he always said he wanted to wait until he was more established and knew we could afford more staff to take on more roles.

How could I possibly say no to this?

I search the house, finding Ellie and Scott looking over plans in the kitchen.

"Hey . . ." I approach them, with a firm grip on the contract.

"So?" Ellie asks, shoving her hands into her overall pockets.

I give a sheepish grin. "I really appreciate the offer . . ." I pause for effect. "And there's no way in hell I would turn it down."

Scott pulls me in for a tight hug. "I'm so glad!"

Ellie hugs me too. "This is so exciting."

"I don't think the world is ready for ElmWoods Contracting and Design to step into the spotlight." I chuckle, handing her my signed contract.

"Who could ever truly mentally prepare for this guy?" She motions a thumb towards Scott.

"*Hey*!"

Ellie smirks at him before turning back to me. "So did you tell her where you're taking her?"

"No. I wasn't sure how to say, 'Hey come to a romantic cottage that my family owns.' Plus, she has enough on her mind now, knowing she'll have to keep this guy in line." I tilt my head towards Scott, igniting a laugh from Ellie.

"Seriously?! Y'all can't gang up on me. It's not fair." Scott fake pouts at Ellie before turning to face me. "Just wait until Whitney is around, she and I can start our own alliance."

We all laugh again.

God, I love my found family, especially since they love Whitney so fiercely.

"Have you decided if you'll stop to see your mom on the way?" Scott asks me.

That's the million-dollar question.

We're going to be passing by Springfield on the way and I know my mom and Wesley are dying to meet Whitney, but I'm not sure if I can work up the courage to ask her yet.

Chapter 32

WHITNEY

The next few days are quiet. Wyatt works late and hasn't been super chatty, so by Friday morning I'm spiraling. Wyatt didn't give me much instruction beyond "pack a suitcase and be ready for anything."

I FaceTime April. "I'm freaking out over here!" I throw my hands up beside my head.

"Hi to you, too." She snickered. "What's going on?"

"Help me pack. I'm about to lose my shit. I'm way too deep in my head right now."

"Okay, show me what you've got so far, and tell me what's going on in your head?"

I tell her about how he's been quieter since I was offered the job and accepted it, before sharing about how nervous I am to spend three days with him in some unknown place and how much I don't want to mess this up.

"Okay, fashion first, then feelings; that's my motto, as of five seconds ago." She smirks at me, and I feel myself let out a loud sigh. "Woman, you need like six outfits a day. Don't pack so lightly. He's whisking you away to some undisclosed location three and a half weeks before Christmas. You bring *alllll* the things," April says, wiggling her eyebrows.

I laugh, opening my closet. "Okay, fair enough."

April spends the next ten minutes telling me what to bring and what not to, while talking me off my emotional ledge. She's my best friend for a million reasons, but her ability to calm my soul in a quick and efficient manner is the most important reason.

Wyatt: I'm here. Want me to come up? Or should I just wait by the truck.

I type back as I walk towards the front door with my stuff.

Whitney: You can wait down there. I'm ready to go.

I lock the door and head downstairs feeling all sorts of butterflies. I have no idea where he's taking me, but honestly, I would follow him anywhere.

I push down the knot in my chest as I see him leaning against his truck with his arms crossed, scanning my body.

He's got a pair of tan pants paired with a dark blue long sleeve shirt, and a small smile on his lips. "Ready?" he asks as he throws my suitcase in the cab of his truck.

"I guess so." I shrug. "It's hard to feel fully prepared when I have no idea where we're going!"

"You'll find out."

"Fine then, be that way." I poke his side before getting in the passenger seat. One of his hats is on the seat.

"Oh sorry. I'll move that." He goes to grab it but before he can take it I put it on my head, matching him by putting it on backwards.

He looks at me wide-eyed. "Whit, you look so hot right now. Dammit." He chuckles. "Hold on." He pulls his phone out and before I can protest has taken a picture of me.

I feel my cheeks flush.

He closes my door and moves towards the driver seat and turns on music for us before setting the truck in motion. I try to think about where he might be taking us. I doubt we're driving more than a few hours.

After almost thirty minutes of silence and me mentally mapping where we're heading to try to discourage the panic from rising in my chest, he turns the music off.

"Sorry I've been quiet . . ." Wyatt says, drumming his fingers on the steering wheel.

I swallow, looking out the window. "Are you regretting asking me to spend the weekend with you?"

He eyes me like that's a crazy thought to have. "No, of course not." He sighs loudly.

"So, what's going on?"

"We're going to be passing Springfield."

Oh. *Oh.*

"You wanna stop and visit your mom?" I ask.

"I don't need to . . . just wasn't sure if you'd want to meet her . . ."

I glance at him through my hair. He's not asking me if I want to meet his mom. He's implying he wants me to, but is leaving it open for me to decide.

This is a big step.

A big deal.

And he knows it.

"I, uh . . . I talk to her about you a lot. Wesley too." My giant teddy bear of a man is looking like a lost lamb, as he stresses himself out.

"Wy, baby. I'd love to meet your family." I grab his upper arm and give it a reassuring squeeze.

"Really?" He sounds excited. "They may not even be home," he says quickly, as if he's trying to back pedal.

"Wyatt Morgan, don't you chicken out on me. I've spent the last half hour thinking you wanted to dump me . . ." I blurt out.

"Wait seriously?!" he replies with a shocked expression.

"Yeah . . ." I sigh nervously.

"Jesus, Whit. You should have told me . . . I feel like an ass right now." He blows air out of his mouth as he thinks. "You thought I was distant the last few days because I wasn't happy for your job, didn't you?"

"Uh . . . Kinda," I stammer.

He eyes me. "I'm really pulling a Scott right now, aren't I?"

I let out a howl of laughter, remembering how frustrated Scott used to make Ellie by playing hot and cold. "Wyatt! I'm going to tell him you said that!"

"Okay, let me start over." Wyatt pinches his nose. "I am so excited that you'll be working at the same office as me, that when I come back from site visits, I'll see you there with a cute dress on, radiating your sunshine everywhere. I decided I wanted you to meet my family the night before you showed up at the house and I lost my nerve and didn't want to overshadow your big news." He frowns at the road. "And I did have to work long days trying to figure out who should take over as head foreman, and since some people are taking vacation around Christmas, we're having a final push on a few things. I want this weekend to be special for you . . . for *us*."

I put my hand on his arm. "You will forever be the best thing that has ever happened to me. When I hug you, it feels like I'm home. I was honestly terrified at the idea of you resenting me."

"I will never ever regret you, Whitney Harris, I promise you that." His voice is so serious it sends a shock right to my core and I'm slapped in the face by a realization . . . *I don't just love him. I'm* in *love with him.*

Now if I can power through my fear long enough to verbalize that to him . . . that would be great.

His Adam's apple bobs as he takes the exit towards Springfield.

"If they aren't home, then I can show you the town," he whispers.

I rest my head on his shoulder and smile; I'm about to see an entire chapter of his life that made him the man he is today.

The town has a cute charm to it. As we pass through downtown Wyatt points out a few places he used to spend time at. When we pull up in front of a house, I smile; there's Christmas decorations lining the outside of the super charming and homey bungalow.

We hop out of the truck and he's smiling ear to ear by the time he gets to the front door. He knocks twice before the front door swings open. His little brother is wide-eyed when he sees him, and they widen all the more when he sees me. "*MA!* Wyatt's here, and he's got a bombshell of a woman with him."

Wyatt swats his brother. "Behave. Jesus, Wesley."

"Hey! Would you have preferred I call her a babe?" He winks at me like some cocky Casanova.

I can't help but laugh watching them interact. I cover my mouth as I see his mom rushing to the door.

"Wyatt!" She hugs him so tightly, sniffling into his chest.

"Hi, Mom. I've missed you," he whispers as he hugs her back. When she pulls back from him, she turns to face me with tears in her eyes. Wyatt has her smile and her dirty blond hair.

She assesses me. "You must be the bombshell!" she jokes with a laugh that echoes into my heart, a laugh that screams, "I'm free from a long reign of hell.", I know it only because it's the kind of laugh Wyatt pries out of me.

"I guess that's me." I laugh, awkwardly. "I'm Whitney."

"Oh, we know!" Wesley says from behind. "Hopefully you can live up to the hype this guy spews at us. I'm surprised you don't have a halo."

Wyatt shoves his brother again and his mom grabs my hand as the guys start trying to put each other in a headlock. "I was just making some tea, come join me? They'll be at this game for a minute or two . . . It happens every time."

"Sure." I nod, following her into the house. It's so clean, and it smells like pine and cinnamon. A Christmas tree is up—half decorated—but I love it, I never had a Christmas tree growing up so knowing that I'll be able to have one this year makes my heart flutter with excitement.

The kitchen is a light blue, similar to Wyatt's house, and everything feels soft and cozy, as if she put a lot of thought into it.

"Would you like some lemon in your tea?" she offers, and I nod again. She passes me a tea mug covered with wildflowers.

Scout's voice enters my head, *Wildflowers are everywhere Whitney, sometimes you just have to look harder to find them.*

I run my fingers along them, tracing the shapes, glad to know my angel is looking down on me, like always. "So, what has Wyatt said about me?" I ask nervously.

His mom places her hand on my arm, and I snap my eyes up to hers and I see a look I've only ever gotten from April, Scout, Ellie, and Wyatt. A look of understanding, a look of pride, a look of compassion.

"He's always had a hard time keeping stuff from me, he's probably told me more about your life than you'd like me to know . . ." She looks down at the walnut kitchen table. "But the admiration he feels towards you is unmatched, Whitney. He talks about you like you built the entire universe. I hear his smile every time he calls me."

I stare at her, mouth open, unsure how to respond.

"You've been through a lot, but I was so glad to see you were so much braver than I knew how to be and finally got out. I know I failed my sons a million times by not leaving their dad, but I know you understand how impossible that feels sometimes."

I rest my other hand on top of hers. "I do. So much . . . but Mrs. Morgan, you didn't fail. Wyatt is so many good things, and I can only assume they're because of *you*. It's hard being stuck in a cycle of abuse. My parents were both raised in houses of abuse. And I definitely have walked into a few situations where I should have known better or seen the neon signs telling me to stay away."

She nods. "You've dealt with a lot for someone so young, and your maturity shows. Wyatt was right about you," she says, sipping her tea.

I readjust my sitting position. "Right in what way?"

"You've got a big heart and you're too hard on yourself."

I let out a genuine laugh. "I may have heard that a time or two before."

We share a sad smile and I decide to shift gears.

"What was Wyatt like as a kid?"

She smiles with the look of pride any mother should have for their child. "He was quiet. Always assessing, always observing . . . always honest. He refused to lie to his dad about anything, which was a bit of an issue at times, but I think it added to the pureness of him. He was a problem solver and a protector. He hasn't changed too much honestly; just a gentle giant who makes me so proud of him every day." Her eyes well up a bit and I feel sad for her. She was innocent once but she walked into a relationship with a man who ended up breaking her apart.

She stands suddenly and walks over to a hutch full of photo albums. She hands me one that says Wyatt James Morgan on the front. I open the front cover and immediately break into giggles. The first picture I see is Wyatt dressed as a fairy princess with chocolate icing all over his face.

"Oh, my goodness." I can't suppress my laugh.

"Mom! Nooooo," Wyatt groans from behind me and I hear Wesley snicker from beside him as they enter the room.

"What, she's gotta see this side of you too. And Wesley, mind your manners or I'll show her yours too." His mom smirks as I scan through the pages. Wyatt was such a cute and smiley kid.

His mom grabs us a few more albums to look through and I spend the better part of the afternoon laughing as the three of them fill the room with such positive energy. Wyatt's little brother is a firecracker, but you can see it in his eye, a glimmer of adoration anytime Wyatt talks. I sit and wonder what they'd all be like if his dad hadn't stolen so much joy from their life for so long.

We spend some time helping his mom decorate more for Christmas and I find myself speaking truthfully about how I never really got to celebrate Christmas growing up and it led to Wyatt's mom assembling a box of Christmas decorations that she wasn't going to use.

I protest, but she refuses to send me home without them. "It's your first Christmas in your own place, you have to have some decorations, Whitney!"

I finally give a slow nod, accepting that she's just being kind and there are no strings attached.

We head out late in the afternoon with the promise of coming back to see them for Christmas. I get a hug from both his mom and brother before we get into the truck and they give us one last wave before going into the house.

Wyatt is sitting with his eyes closed, as if he is replaying a movie in his mind. He exhales and turns the key. I can tell he wants silence, that his brain is loud and busy right now, so I watch the cars passing by us, I watch the roads shift between us. I watch the trees and I wait.

I would wait a lifetime for him if he needed it.

Chapter 33

WHITNEY

After almost ten minutes of silence, he lets out a long breath and whispers, "Thank you," and my heart melts because his tone is vulnerable—unsure of himself.

I stare out the front window, afraid to look at him and blurt out the words exploding inside my soul. Instead, I say, "Your brother looks just like you."

"Yeah, he'll be fighting the ladies off with sticks for the rest of his life."

I look around the truck and say, "Hmm, I don't see any ladies with sticks in here, you've lost your touch I guess."

Wyatt chuckles. "Nah, I've got this force field around me, and it's named Whitney."

I turn to face him, admire him. He's focused on the road, and he seems at peace. "I'm glad you introduced me to them. They're really special."

You're really special.

We drive past a small town I've never heard of before and I watch as we pull down a dirt road. I stare at him in confusion as we reach a cottage overlooking a bright blue lake.

"Do you have another relative you're expecting me to meet?" I bite my lip.

"Nope. This belonged to my grandparents and their siblings; we grew up coming here. When my grandpa died, my mom and her sister got ownership of it. We get it for half the year, they get it the other half."

I unbuckle my seatbelt as I take in the peacefulness.

"I'll get the bags and the food out of the car, you go sit by the water if you want."

"I can help you. It's okay . . ." I offer.

He kisses my forehead. "I know you can, but you've done enough already. You go check the water temperature." He opens the back door of the truck. I head around the side of the cottage and gasp. There's a midsized pool and jacuzzi and a sprawling deck overlooking the lake. There's some boats and fishing gear by the sandy shore. I slip my foot out of my boot and dip one toe into the water and sigh. It's cold, but the stress of the day and the warmth in my heart make it more tolerable.

I move around the outer perimeter of the cottage; it's a gorgeous property, large oak trees surrounding the space. When I walk into the kitchen through the back door I nod as I take in the layout and arrangement, seeing familiar touches of Scott's handiwork. "Ah . . . you guys redid this place, didn't you?" I ask Wyatt, who is currently putting snacks into the fridge.

"Maybe."

"I love it! Ellie would die if she saw these beams." I laugh, staring up at the ceiling.

"You feel like going for a swim?" Wyatt asks me.

"In which of the three options?" I retort, with a laugh.

He smirks. "Whichever you decide. I'll show you to the room and you can change while I finish unpacking everything down here."

I follow him down the hall to a room with a king-sized bed covered in a dark gray comforter. My suitcase is on one side of the bed and attached to our room is a large bathroom. I open my bag and pull out a navy blue bikini, throwing my hair into a bun before brushing my teeth. I weigh my options for which body of water is preferred. Definitely not the lake, I don't need to freeze, so I decide to head to the jacuzzi.

I hop into the warm water and sigh. My eyes shut as a contented feeling takes over my body.

The only noise is the leaves rustling in the wind.

A kiss lands on the back of my neck, and I squeal. "You startled me."

"I'm good at that, huh?"

Wyatt places a lemonade in the cup holder beside me and then hops over the edge, sitting across from me. My cheeks flush as I watch his naked torso settle itself into the water.

"What?" Wyatt smirks at me.

I roll my eyes at him. "Nothing."

"Tell me."

I sigh. "I read a book recently that had a hot tub ordeal." I look off to the side.

Wyatt chuckles. I want to tell him he feels too far away, that there's too much empty space between us, but I don't want him to think I'm trying to force sex or something.

"Yeah? And what exactly is a *hot tub ordeal*?" His tone is full of amusement.

I bite my lip. "Just some kissing," I say quickly.

Wyatt moves towards me and brings his lips to mine and I suddenly feel desperate for him.

He pulls back, kissing my neck. "And?"

"And what?" I pant, trying to hide my frustration at him ending the kiss.

He rubs his lips across my jaw. "I assume there's more to this *ordeal*, or have you started reading clean romance novels?" he teases, running his finger across my collar bone.

"They have sex, okay . . ." I say.

"Baby, if you want to have hot tub sex with me you don't need to make up some fake story." He gives me a cocky smile.

"Oh, shut up." I groan through my smile.

His fingers run across my chest now. "I don't think navy blue is your color, I think we need to get rid of this." With his other hand, he unties my bathing suit from around my neck.

I bite my lip as his hand moves to the strings behind my back, freeing my breasts.

"I've missed these beautiful gals so much." Wyatt grabs each of them in his hands, eagerly.

"You're so lame," I try to say with a straight face, but his fingers move across my skin and my body melts into his.

"Whit, you're interrupting my joyous reunion here." Wyatt gives me a cocky smile and I can't help but laugh. "Where was I . . ." He strokes my nipples and I let out a moan. "Ah, right there, yes."

Wyatt hoists me up and spins me around so I can settle onto his lap.

His hands move over my body slowly and I kiss him hard, urgently. His body awakens below me, and we cling to each other. "Where's the closest condom?" I whisper.

He laughs and lifts up my untouched drink, pulling a condom out from under it.

"Crafty fella, aren't you?" I tease, standing up.

He smirks at me as I shimmy out of my bottoms.

"You think you're getting lucky, don't you?"

"Baby, you're saying that to me . . . while naked. So yeah, I kinda think so."

He puts the condom on and slips me back onto his lap, both of us sighing happily as I settle around him.

We're touching each other in every possible way until we both come undone.

His thumb brushes my cheek, and he shakes his head as he looks down at me. "You are everything to me."

Chapter 34

WYATT

I sneak out of bed hesitantly, not really wanting to leave her but also needing a moment to myself. Whitney met my brother. And my mom. I've never brought a girl home before and I'm glad that it was *her* that got the honor to be first. And honestly, I'm hoping she's the last one too.

Seeing her laugh with my mom, seeing her eyes light up when she skimmed through the family pictures . . . It made my heart glow.

I love her so much. I've known it for a while now, there's this pull towards her, one that makes me want to do cliché rom-com movie grand gestures. Maybe not the whole break out in song and jazz hands shit but I wish I could scream, "I love you," from the rooftop.

But I also know for a fact that she's only ever said it to three people in her life: April, Scout, and Ellie. I'm an "I love you" person, so I say it to so many people; probably because I spent the better part of seventeen years thinking my dad might kill me, my mom, or Wesley.

I sit on the dock watching the sunrise and let out a contented sigh. I have a feeling this will be the best Christmas and December I've had in my entire life.

I hear the patio door open and Whitney approaches.

"Morning, Wy," she says sleepily. She's got thick socks on her feet and a large blanket wrapped around her tightly.

"How'd my girl sleep?" I ask her.

"Good," she says quietly.

"Are you okay?" I try to bring her towards me, but she drops the blanket, stepping back from me. She's naked except for her socks. She bites her lip then lays the blanket on the dock and raises an eyebrow at me.

"Goddamn it, Whitney," I mumble, standing up. "I don't have a condom on me."

She leans down and pulls one out of her sock and I can't help but laugh at her quick thinking. It's a bit chilly this morning but the warmth of our bodies collide and I fall into her easily. Something about this feels different, and not because my ass is cold. She's looking into my eyes and keeps whispering how perfect I am—how much I mean to her—while I savor every inch of her.

After a shower to warm ourselves up, I build us a fire and grab my guitar before settling down onto the cottage floor.

Whitney's grin is infectious as I strum the guitar. She lowers herself onto the ground beside me.

"Sing with me?" I ask her.

"Of course."

We sing a few songs together before she grabs my arm.

"What's up?"

"I was hoping you could teach me how to play . . ." She motions her head towards the guitar.

"Really?" I can't hide my excitement. I pull her between my legs and put the guitar in front of us.

She leans back against me as I show her how to position her fingers for E minor. She strums a few times and squeals with excitement. I walk her through a few chords before she turns to face me. "I want you to teach me how to play 'Yours.'"

Two hours later, Whitney has really started to get the hang of the chords to the song. And when she tells me to sit on the couch, and she sits in front of me with the guitar in her lap, my heart feels full.

"Bear with me here," she says quickly before diving into the song.

I'm quick to understand why people swoon over someone playing an instrument for them.

Especially when they are watching you like you are the most important person in their life.

When she finishes singing, I can't contain myself. I slide the guitar off her lap and pull her against me, kissing her. "That was incredible, Whitney."

She pulls back and her green eyes are damp.

"What's wrong?" I ask her, quickly wiping a tear from her cheek.

"Nothing. I . . ." Whitney takes a long breath. "I love you."

It takes a moment for the words to sink in.

Her cheeks flush. "I'm sorry if it's too soon. I'm sorry if you don't feel the same way. I just . . . I needed to say it."

A single tear falls down her cheek, as I let out a long laugh and I see confusion cross her face.

"What?" she asks, self-consciously crossing her arms.

My eyes scan her face for a moment before I lean my forehead against hers. "You beat me to it. Same way you kissed me on our first date." I let out a long exhale before adding, "I love you so goddamn much, Whitney Harris. I think I loved you from the minute you walked into my life."

She stares at me still, like a deer in headlights. "Really?"

I tilt her chin up to me and whisper, "More than words, my little wildflower."

Chapter 35

WHITNEY

Everything is feeling really good, especially since April and Wyatt get along well. I've convinced both of them to come riding with me today, though neither of them required much convincing. Turns out Wyatt loves riding as much as we do.

April opens the gate with a giant smile. "I've missed you, roomie," she says before hugging me. I let out a long laugh, considering I saw her at sewing class two nights ago.

Wyatt and I move inside the arena where the horses are already prepared and waiting for us.

"I'm just glad I get to ride horses with my two favorite people today!" I reply as the two of them hug.

"Apparently Jeff is excited to be reunited with Wyatt," April says with a wink as she tugs on my braids.

I tug hers back before brushing Ronald's mane. Wyatt beelines for Jeff and starts petting her face.

April whispers, "Damn. Wyatt is meant to be a cowboy, isn't he?"

I giggle and peek over at him, he's dressed in faded jeans, a plaid shirt, and a faded cowboy hat. I almost didn't make it out of the apartment because I was way too hot and bothered by the sight of him.

"Yes, he really is." I lean my head against Ronald's and sigh.

"Okay, love eyes away for a minute," April teases. "Let's see if we can still jump these horses."

I went easy on Wyatt the first time we came riding, but April and I can be quite competitive. She had a dream of racing horses and jumping until Scout died.

The three of us lead the horses to the arena and April gives me a coy smile. "Warm up time?"

I snicker. "You betcha."

Before Wyatt can process what we're doing, April and I take off into a canter, leaving Wyatt and Jeff in our dust.

"Oh, come on! No fair!" he shouts with a chuckle.

April's horse and mine move in tandem, familiar with our need to show off after all these years. To my surprise, the sound of hooves approach me on my left. Wyatt flashes a cocky smile, tilting his head down into a nod. "Never underestimate Jeff and her need to be the best!"

April and I chuckle as Wyatt passes us, and to our surprise, leads Jeff over a jump.

I slow Ronald down to a trot as Wyatt does a victory lap.

"Okay, show off," April calls out. "We're just getting started!"

"You're so on." Wyatt brings Jeff to a stop beside us, shooting me a quick wink as he tips his cowboy hat.

Jesus.

I don't think the horse is the only thing I'll be riding tonight.

The door closes behind us and I press him against the wall, tugging on his belt. Wyatt smiles against my lips as he puts his hat on the side table and lifts me into his arms, carrying us to the couch.

I can't move my hands quick enough, undoing every button on his shirt frantically.

"What's gotten into you?" Wyatt chuckles, resting his hands on my hips.

"*You.* In a cowboy hat." I place the hat back on his head before sliding his shirt down his shoulders and arms, running my hands over his chest.

He moves quickly and flops me down on his oversized couch, sliding my pants down my legs. I move to sit up, but he shakes his head.

"Not yet." He kneels in front of the couch, running a hand over my black silk underwear. His finger grazes across the top of my underwear and I moan. He's watching my face as his fingers dance across my skin.

He slides my shirt up over my head, kissing his way up my stomach as his hand snakes around my back to unhook my bra, and a sigh of relief leaves my lips.

He chuckles. "Weight off your shoulders?"

"Literally," I respond.

He motions for me to sit up and I do. If he asked me to jump right now, I'd say how high. He stands there gawking down at me as if he hasn't seen me naked countless times already.

"Whitney . . . look at me." I look into his brown eyes, his face is serious. "You are a *fucking* goddess."

"Enough of that sweet talking. Take your pants off, dammit!" I giggle in response. "And get a condom on," I tell him.

He nods, moving into his pants for his wallet. He rolls it on at record speed and I stand up in front of him, pushing him onto the couch before straddling him.

I move my hips slowly at first but when his hands find my breasts, my orgasm nudges its way closer to the surface. He's staring at me as if he's dreamed of this moment his whole life, which only makes me more aroused. I roll my body, clutching onto his strong shoulders as I pick up my pace. "That's my beautiful girl, come undone for me," he whispers against my ear. It's enough to send me over the edge, moaning as I collapse onto his shoulder, letting my orgasm roll through me.

He kisses my neck. "I love you."

"God, I love you too," I say once I catch my breath.

"Roll over," he tells me. I nod slowly.

He pulls me off of him, turning me so I'm on all fours.

He brushes his lips across my waist before entering me again. I moan instantly.

"Ready?" Hh whispers.

I roll my eyes. "For what?"

His hand caresses my ass and then he digs his fingers into my hips, hard enough to ensure I don't move. His movement is hard and fast; he's filling me up. I find my back arching towards him, craving every part of him. When he says, "Come for me, Whitney," and presses his thumb down on my clit I feel myself erupt in ways I never have before.

I barely hear the sound of the front door open as I sit staring numbly at the front page of today's paper. "Sorry I'm late, work was hectic today," Wyatt calls out.

"Whitney?" His voice sounds far away, even though the shadow of his body fills my peripheral vision. "What's wrong? What happened?"

I don't know how to answer him so instead I point to the coffee table.

He looks down and gasps.

I don't need to see the headline again; I've already read it way too many times.

Attempted bank robbery was avoided after a brave bank clerk stepped in, knocking the gun out of the robber's hand.

A picture of a man, who looks barely older than me, is beside the headline, but two lines down in the article my mother's name stares back at me.

Karen Harris, arrested.

I had called my lawyer when I first saw it and sure enough, with video evidence and her previous record, my mother is going away.

Wyatt sits down on the couch beside me, opening and closing his mouth a few times, as if he's trying to figure out what to say.

"Deacon was her getaway driver," I tell him, my eyes not meeting his. "They mention him later in the article. He's been arrested too."

We both sit in silence for a long time before I shift, looking towards Wyatt.

My eyes burn. "I don't know why I'm even sad right now."

Wyatt grabs my hands and lets out a quiet sigh. "Yes, you do. She was your mom—a terrible one, but she was a part of your life for longer than anyone else. She formed the best parts of you. She made you empathetic, hardworking, and pure. She taught you what *not* to be. And then April and Scout taught you what *to* be. It's normal for you to not want someone to rot in jail, but Whitney, she deserves to be there for everything she did to you. For trying to rob a bank. None of that was okay."

I nod. "I think I need to cry about it."

Wyatt pulls me against him, letting me sob into his shoulder. My cries are loud, as if I'm releasing twenty-four years of pent-up emotions.

When I pull away, my eyes are puffy. My hand falls to his chest, feeling for Wyatt's heartbeat.

My calming presence.

My family.

Chapter 36

WYATT

"I'm thinking I want to get a cat or something," Whitney tells me as I place a grilled cheese sandwich onto her plate.

"Yeah? That would be fun," I reply, sitting across from her at the table. "What kind would you want?"

"I always wanted the mini munchkin ones with the short legs, but I know they're hard to find. So whatever cat at the shelter meshes with me best . . . and warms up to you too." Her cheeks redden slightly as she says it.

I reach across the table and let my hand graze hers. "Didn't Ronald and Jeff teach you anything? Animals love me."

Her laughter is loud. "Wanna come meet cats with me today? Maybe see if there's one that will be a good fit for us?"

"Absolutely. I always wanted to get a dog or a cat, but I always worry with my long days that I'd need something super low maintenance."

"You can be the dad to my cat," I say and instantly feel my cheeks go red. "Uh . . . that sounded weird and I'm not trying to make you sign up for something you don't have an interest in . . ."

I graze her pinky with a mischievous smile on my lips. "I think it would be good practice."

"F-for what?" she chews her lip, anxiously.

"For when we have kids someday, silly. I mean . . . if you want them too."

"I do." Her jaw hangs open as my eyes find hers.

"I've seen the future, Whitney, and it includes some mini-Whitney's with the greenest eyes. I just thought you should know . . . I'm in this forever."

"You'd want to have kids with me? What if I . . . What if I turn into my mom . . ."

I move around the table and sit next to her. "That will never happen, and you know it. You're going to be too busy loving them to hurt them like that, and I will be too."

We share a sad smile before finally Whitney looks up at me and touches the side of my face. "You'd be the best dad in the world, Wy."

"Well, let's go find a cat and test that theory, why don't we!" I say, walking towards the front door.

We end up going to Healing Hearts Animal Rescue and the giddiness on Whitney's face is all consuming. She's on the floor in seconds, petting any kitten and cat that surrounds her.

"How will I ever choose?" she huffs out, looking around the room.

I get down on the floor with her and a caramel-colored kitten finds its way onto my lap, purring louder than any of the other cats in the room. Whitney giggles and takes a photo of me with the cat.

"You look cute with a cat in your lap! Especially since she's the color of your eyes!" she exclaims.

"I do, don't I?" I joke back to her, continuing to pet the kitten's soft fur.

"I think we found our winner," Whitney says matter-of-factly.

"We don't know if she or he likes you though . . ." I reply, with a raised eyebrow.

Whitney comes towards me and pets the cat in my lap, checking her collar. "Doesn't matter; she has good taste, and her fur matches your eyes, what else is there to know?"

"Her name?" I prompt.

Whitney just laughs. "I'm so glad you asked, it's Roger."

"Is it actually?" I reach towards the collar and read the tag which says, "Unnamed." Whitney is smirking at me. It's impossible not to find her charming, especially when the kitten moves out of my lap and into hers.

"Well, Roger, let's get you home before someone comes along and tries to give a name like Whiskers or Stella!"

Whitney gives the kitten one last pet and gets her palm licked before standing up. "The horror, we can't let that happen."

Twenty minutes later, papers are signed, and Roger is ours.

We stop at the pet store on our way home and Whitney fills up the cart with all sorts of toys and cat treats, radiating pure joy.

When we get back to the apartment, Whitney gives the cat a long tour of every room in the house and then sets up the food and litter area.

And then Whitney turns around and faces me with a devilish smile. "What?"

"It's like two weeks until Christmas, I think we should decorate!"

"I love that idea."

"Are we . . . uh . . . doing gifts for Christmas?" She pops her lip into her mouth nervously.

"Whit, I bought your gift weeks ago, there's no way I'd not spoil my girl, especially on our first Christmas together!"

Her smile widens as she hugs herself against me. "Okay, I didn't want to assume . . . I never really got gifts from my mom or Deacon, obviously."

I kiss her forehead. "Well, this year is going to be different."

"I love you so much." Whitney lets out a contented sigh.

"I love you too, my little wildflower."

Meowing brings our attention to Roger and we both laugh. Crouching to pet her, I add, "Oh, don't worry. We love you too, Roger!"

Chapter 37

WYATT

Whitney is standing outside the office when I arrive, wearing a green jumpsuit and a jean jacket. She smiles at the sight of me. "Merry Christmas Eve!" she calls out as she pulls open the door.

I lean in, kissing her. "Are you ready for our first Christmas together?"

"Yes! I've been waiting my entire life for it."

"Trust me, I'm hoping it can be one you'll always remember . . . I'm hoping it makes up for all the Christmases you missed out on." I give her thigh a quick squeeze before we head towards her place, singing along to Christmas Carols.

Once we get to her apartment, I tell her to head upstairs alone so I can get her gift out of the back without her peeking.

"Fine!" She fake pouts before walking away from me, humming "We Wish You a Merry Christmas" under her breath.

I pull my overnight bag out of the trunk before grabbing the wrapped gift from the backseat and heading inside.

I may have gone a bit overboard for her, but I wanted her to feel completely spoiled today.

When I reach her floor, she's got her door propped open a bit.

I nudge it open with my shoulder and can't hide my smile as I look at her apartment. After we brought Roger back to her place, we really leaned into the Christmas spirit, decorating every possible surface and making our way through as many holiday movies as humanly possible. Her apartment looks like holiday spirit threw up in here, in the best way possible. It reminds me of how much effort my mom put into making our home festive at holidays. The only addition I haven't seen is a stack of gifts under the tree.

Whitney is leaning against the island fidgeting with her hands.

I put her gift box down on the table and pull her against me. "Are you okay?"

She hugs me tightly, and mumbles something into my chest.

It makes me chuckle. "Baby, I got absolutely none of that!"

She leans her head back, and her voice is pleading as she says, "Can we do gifts now? I don't think I can wait until morning."

"A bit impatient?" I tease, leaning my forehead against hers. But I'm sure she realizes I'm also feeling impatient.

"Wy, I've never done this, I feel like I should cram twenty-four years into one day. I'm trying not to be a giddy mess or overeager . . . but it's hard not to." She gives an awkward laugh.

"Well, let's open these gifts then!" I reply, moving towards the living room.

Whitney follows me, but hovers by the side of the couch.

"Baby." I chuckle again, giving her a lopsided smile. "I know this is new to you, but if there's a certain way you want to do things, you gotta tell me."

Whitney exhales a long breath and then sits down on the floor in front of the tree, patting the floor beside her.

I grab her gift and sit on the floor so I'm facing her, smiling as Roger comes to join us. "So, how do you want to do this?"

She chews the inside of her cheek. "You go first ... I mean, you open your gift from me first," she says quickly, handing me a card.

I smile as I read the words My Wy-ld Flower on the envelope that is also covered in hand-drawn flowers and butterflies wearing Santa hats.

Dammit, that might be the cutest thing I've ever seen.

I open the card and read her words.

Wyatt,

Merry Christmas.

When I met your friends for the first time, Frankie called me the wild card, but he was wrong. You were the wild card. You were the wildflower in a world of thorns and pain. I want you to know how much you changed my life and how grateful I am for this life. You make me better than I was before.

I cannot imagine my life without you. You are everything to me.

Love always,
Whitney

I wipe a tear from the corner of my eye and meet her eyes. "Whitney Harris, you little wordsmith, you."

She gives a coy smile, handing me a gift bag. "This first!"

Inside the bag is a framed photo of us from when we went camping with our flower crowns on and the movie White Christmas—the movie Wesley, my mom, and I would always watch on Christmas Eve. On the front of the movie is a sticky note that says:

Old traditions with new people?

"Whitney, this is so sweet!" I pull her into me, kissing her hard. "I love it so much."

She picks up another, smaller wrapped gift and extends it to me with shaky hands.

"Whitney, you didn't have to spoil me," I exclaim, as she places the box in my hand.

She nods, wiping tears that are starting to fall. "Yes I did. I can't repay you for all the joy you've brought me these past few months, and how strong you've helped me become." She places the gift in my hand.

I unwrap it to find a box and when I open it, a key falls into my lap.

"Roger and I had a chat . . . We figured you were here often enough already that you might as well have your own key. I'm not asking you to move in, but if you end up spending days at a time here, that's okay. I won't say you need to leave, and if you want a drawer or something for clothes, I have space," she whispers nervously, watching for my reaction.

I reach into my pocket and pull out my keychain, adding it onto it. "This is the best gift I've ever received."

Her body relaxes and you can see relief fill her eyes. "Okay. I didn't want to overwhelm you and make you feel like I was being needy . . ."

"Trust me, Whitney, I'll move in one sock at a time if I need to, but at some point, and it could be a month from now or a year from now, you and I are going to live together and start building our life together," I promise her.

Her smile reaches her eyes as I slide the gift that I brought between us and place the card on top. "Your turn."

She opens the card and very quickly her eyes fill with tears.

She hugs the card to her chest and then places it beside her. Moving towards the gift, she unwraps it slowly, as if she's trying to savor this moment. But when the sewing machine comes into view, she loses it; tears pour out of her eyes in rapid succession. "H-h-how?" Her green eyes are wide and she's shaking.

"I asked April if she knew the name of the sewing machine Scout owned and then she and I did some hunting at antique stores . . . Paige ended up saving the day and found this available at a store an hour away, so I took a road trip a few weeks ago while you had a girls' day with Ellie and April."

"And you tell me that I'm sneaky, huh?" Her eyes are shining as she runs her hand over the box.

"We don't know for certain if it'll run, but we figure between all of us, someone might be handy enough to fix it."

Whitney picks the box up and carries it to the desk in her room, taking the machine out the packaging.

The sewing machine is a dark purple with etched wildflowers on it, it goes so well with her room. And it suits Whitney.

She runs her hand over it and closes her eyes. "I didn't expect meeting you to give me closure on losing Scout too, but somehow it has. You healed so many parts of me."

Chapter 38

WHITNEY

Today marks a new chapter and I can't hide my smile as I walk towards the front door.

A banner that says: **NOW OPEN** hangs from the front window, right under the ElmWoods Contracting and Design sign on the building. Ellie and Scott have two very different styles, but Paige was able to capture a perfect balance of feminism and masculinity in the font choice.

Seeing their trademark front door color on the sign and the front door warms my heart.

Everyone cheers as we enter the office space which has balloons and streamers scattered throughout the office space.

I'm excited to finally see the finished result. It's been just over a month since they started renovating the space—which became the highlight of season two of *From The Ground Up*—turning our new office space into their dream work space.

It includes big windows to let ample sunlight shine through, elm flooring, larger workspaces, and soft colors throughout. I spent the last two weeks helping Paige organize and set everything up. It's been a flurry of chaos, but I'm leaning into the saying, "New Year, New Me."

I was giddy when I found out that Wyatt and Grant's office would be right beside mine. Even though they'll be out on-site visits, the prospect of having the occasional lunch date with Wyatt excites me. When Paige and I set up their space, I was sure to print off a few photos of Wyatt and I to add to the space. On Grant's desk, Paige had placed a photo of Wyatt from the fundraiser, with his purple butterfly face. The frame says **My Work Wife** and right beside it is a picture of Bree. Paige and I had a long laugh about it, knowing that Grant will get a kick out of it.

The only office I haven't seen completely finished yet is mine. Ellie had let me pick out the color palettes and wood tones I'd like included so I've been eager to see the end result; though she has a long track record of knowing exactly what I like.

As I walk towards reception, where Wyatt stands with a lopsided grin, he gives me a quick wave. "Welcome to ElmWoods Contracting and Design, my name is Wyatt Morgan, Project Manager extraordinaire." He extends his hand to me professionally and everybody chuckles.

I just roll my eyes at him as Ellie and Paige approach us.

Paige winks at me. "Ready to see your new digs?"

"Heck yes." I reply, before pointing a finger at the three of them. "No tears this time though, right?"

Ellie just shrugs and says, "We have no say in your reaction, Whitney," as they motion for me to open the only closed office door.

"You go ahead, okay?" Wyatt prompts me as they take a step back.

I open the door and my eyes widen as I take in my surroundings.

The room is painted a light purple, with canvases of painted butterflies lining the wall. Beside that is a cork board that has pictures of me and my friends and a few of Wyatt and I.

It looks exactly how I pictured it. I absolutely love it.

My tears quickly flow as I look at the picture on my desk of Scout and I, with a plate full of pancakes in front of us. Beside it is the last note that she wrote to me before she died, framed. The words ***"Wildflowers are everywhere, but you will always be mine. xx Scout"*** make my heart flip-flop.

I sit down at my desk and run my fingers across the words.

Wyatt falls into the chair across from me, offering me a gentle smile. "I love the aesthetic of your office. I might need to stop by from time to time."

I let out a laugh. "Well, I'm sure Grant will be all sorts of willing to write you up."

"I don't doubt that," Wyatt replies, snorting. "You like your office though?"

I nod, taking in my surroundings again. "Yes. Seriously, this is too much. I don't deserve this."

"Nah, my little wildflower, you definitely deserve this." He extends a hand towards me and I take it eagerly.

"I love you," I tell him.

"I love you too, Whitney. Now c'mon, it's time to cut the cake!"

We head out of my office into the main space. People are standing around holding champagne flutes, and Paige hands me and Wyatt each a glass of non-alcoholic champagne, "We got the fancy cups today!" she exclaims before continuing to hand drinks out to everyone else.

Ellie and Scott hold hands at the front of the room, beaming as they look around at everybody.

Scott clears his throat, causing everyone to look towards himself and Ellie.

"I'm going to get started here before I get emotional . . ." Ellie starts, her lips already wobbling. "This is a big change for everybody, and it might take time to learn new faces, or new job titles, but Scott and I are just so grateful to each and every one of you for being on this journey with us, it has been a pleasure blending our worlds together, and we have so many things to look forward to. You are not just our employees, but you are our family. And we love you all." Her eyes are watering as she raises her cup, looking directly at me when she says, "To found family."

Everyone clinks their glasses together before taking a drink.

When I meet Wyatt's eye he holds up his cup and whispers, "To love."

Without missing a beat, I reply, "To the people who build me up."

The End.

Epilogue

WYATT - 1½ YEARS LATER

I stand at the front of the church, anxiety filling my lungs. Wesley is standing beside me with all the other groomsmen. Scott and Frankie are both tearing up already, so I flash them a look, as if to say, *"Don't you start."*

I've been anxiously waiting for this moment since the day I proposed to Whitney.

We start the day like we usually do, snuggled up in bed with Roger, and make pancakes for breakfast before I tell her we're going on a quick drive. But when I pull up in front of Scout's old farm, she meets me with a confused expression. April and I had approached the new homeowner a few months earlier, asking if I could use their property to propose. The couple were moved by the idea and didn't hesitate before saying yes.

"What are we doing here?" Whitney asks as she hops out of my truck.

"I want a tour." I wink, keeping my tone casual.

Her eyes are wide as she takes in the space, and I know she's being brought back to a lifetime of memories.

"They've kept most things the same . . ." She clutches her heart as we walk up the path towards the barn. She points from one thing to the next telling me all about moments she shared with April and Scout and her eyes well with tears as she talks.

We make it to a bench overlooking the garden of flowers and she sits down.

"Thank you for bringing me here. It would be her ninetieth birthday today, you know?"

"Yes, August sixth will be a national holiday in the Morgan household for the rest of our lives . . . A cause for celebration, you might say."

She looks at me with confusion. "What?"

I kneel in front of her, and she gasps. "Whitney, I love you and I want you to be my wife. I want us to chase our dreams together; create a life together." I pull the ring out of my pocket and smile as she takes in the silver band with a diamond shining back at her. "Marry me?"

Her hand extends towards mine, as her eyes lock on mine as tears start to form. "Oh my god, yes! Of course!"

I place the ring on her finger with shaky hands.

"This is so beautiful," she gushes as she stares at her ring and as we pull each other into a hug we both can't help but laugh when a butterfly lands on her hand.

I guess I have Scout's seal of approval.

I readjust my tie as the music changes to a piano version of "My Girl" and everybody takes a seat.

Slowly the doors open at the back of the church and Ellie moves down the aisle in a lavender colored dress. Her eyes are watery when she reaches me.

She gives me a nod before standing across from Scott, he gives her a subtle wink as Bree reaches the front of the church.

Paige is next down the aisle, her hair dyed lavender to match her dress. She'd spent the last few weeks trying to convince me to also dye my hair to match her.

When she passes me, she whispers, "Still think you should have gone with the purple hair; would have really tied everything together."

I chuckle, shaking my head before turning my attention to April making her way down the aisle now, tears flowing freely.

When she reaches me, she gives me a tight hug. "I guess we're officially family now," I tell her, before passing her a tissue.

She wipes her tears, squeezing my hand. "We were family from the minute she fell in love with you, you know that. We're family for life."

The pastor instructs everyone to stand and my heart flutters in anticipation.

The doors open for the last time, and I look towards her. Her eyes are downcast, and similar to the night we first met, she looks up at me slowly, her green eyes captivating me. It feels like we're both looking up for the first time in our lives.

My mom stands beside Whitney, a total mess, as she clings to her arm.

I was beyond humbled when Whitney told me she wanted my mom to walk her down the aisle. In the last year, they've gotten extra close and continued to heal each other in ways I never could have expected. After Wesley got accepted to Vanderbilt University for social work, my mom decided it was time for her to move back to Nashville, and Whitney was her biggest cheerleader and support throughout the first few months.

The two of them have formed an unbreakable bond.

The kind of bond she should have had with her own mother all along.

When they reach the front of the church they share a long hug, and I hear Whitney whisper, "I love you, *Mom*," making a tear fall from my eyes. No matter how many times she's said it, it always feels like the first time.

My mom hugs me. "You did good, Wyatt. I'm so proud of you."

As my mom moves towards the pews, I finally allow myself to look over at Whitney in her strapless gown—the one she made herself, using the sewing machine I got her for our first Christmas together. She's paired it with the veil that April wore on her own wedding day . . . the one Scout wore on hers.

"Hi, almost husband, you look handsome," she whispers as she grabs my hand.

"You look breathtaking," I reply, rubbing my finger along her pinky.

The pastor starts to speak but I don't hear a word he's saying, I'm too busy staring at my future wife.

My wildflower.

We chose to keep our vows simple, for the sake of neither of us wanting to end up as blubbering messes– though at this point, I think we're going to fail miserably anyway.

She goes first.

I, Whitney, take you, Wyatt, to be my husband.

I promise to love you unconditionally,

and listen, for as long as it takes for you to feel heard.

I promise to take you horseback riding at least once a month,

And fill your days with laughter, music, and make you cinnamon pancakes.

I promise to bring out the best in you, because you bring out the best in me.

I exhale before speaking.

I, Wyatt, take you, Whitney, to be my wife.

I promise to love you unconditionally.

To listen, for as long as it takes for you to feel heard.

I promise to play guitar for you at least once a month,

And to fill your days with new book recommendations, grilled cheese sandwiches, and endless Roger cuddles.

I promise to bring out the best in you, because you bring out the best in me.

We exchange rings with tears in our eyes.

Our pastor motions for us to face the crowded church before saying, "And so now, by the power vested in me by the state of Tennessee, it is my honor and delight to declare you husband and wife. Please join me in celebrating Mr. and Mrs. Wyatt and Whitney Morgan. You may seal this declaration with a kiss."

Whitney presses her lips to mine before whispering, "I guess happy endings do exist, huh?"

"They do. But this isn't the ending, Whitney; it's only the beginning."

Bonus Epilogue

Whitney - Five Years Later

The sun is starting to set as our daughter, Scout, runs wild in the yard with our dog, Napoleon, chasing behind her. I lean against the porch banister feeling completely at peace. The past five years have been incredible. Getting married, having our daughter and redoing a farmhouse not far from the property April's grandma had owned was a whirlwind but a dream come true.

Wyatt changed my life in a much bigger way than I expected, and every day is better than the one before. Sometimes I forget how trauma formed my life for years, how my mother broke me time and time again. That world feels so far away now. Knowing my mother is in prison and will never be able to poison my children or get in my head is freeing in so many ways.

"Scout, come wash up, ya turkey. It's almost dinner time," I call out, stepping off the back porch.

Scout continues to twirl around. "Cinnamon pancakes or grilled cheese? What about grilled cheese pancakes?"

"We might need to try that someday. But I'm just craving cinnamon pancakes tonight, if that's okay?" I reply with a smile. "I'll even let you lick the spoon, now come along, silly girl!"

"In a minnuteeee!" she exclaims, throwing another stick for Napoleon. I move down another step, only pausing when I hear the screen door pop open behind me.

"Hey now, you sit." Wyatt grabs me and rubs my belly for the billionth time today. "We've got another week before Thomas comes; I've got her. Rest." He kisses my head before bringing both his arms over his head, roaring like a monster as he chases Scout around the yard. Her squeals bring tears to my eyes.

I'd blame the pregnancy hormones, but watching Wyatt become a dad has been my favorite thing to witness so far. Knowing our kids never have to worry about being abused or feeling unloved means everything to me. Scout idolizes him and he loves her so fiercely. When she was born, his face said it all; he would love her unconditionally.

The way he loves me.

I sit down on the porch swing, the baby kicking with each sway of the swing. "Not much longer . . ." I hold my belly, cherishing this moment—this life. Everything I never expected to have.

Scout is dragging Wyatt towards the steps with determination on her face. "Daddy told me something."

"Oh? What did he tell you?"

"That he loves you more than chocolate cake." She sits down beside me, leaning against my belly.

I laugh, running a hand through her long blonde hair. "Wow, I'm so lucky."

Wyatt sits down on the swing beside us.

"I love you," I tell our daughter as I stare into her caramel eyes, that mirror Wyatt's. "You are such a gift, Scout April Harris, I'm so grateful to be your mom."

Scout looks up at me, beaming. "You're the best mommy in the whole wide world!"

Wyatt's hand lands on top of mine. "I'm also very grateful for your mom."

"Why is that, daddy?" Scout asks, innocently.

"Well, beyond the fact that she brought you into the world, she made me become the best version of myself. She's the best gift I could ever have . . . besides you of course."

Scout nods, resting her hand on my belly. The baby kicks and Scout leans her head against my belly. "What's that, little brother?" she mumbles against my stomach for a minute while Wyatt and I try to keep a straight face. She pops her head up and turns to me. "He says you are his best gift in life too. He says that you make everyone's life better and he can't wait to meet you."

She then looks towards Wyatt. "He also says you have the most soothing voice he's ever heard in his life; he'll expect many lullabies from you."

I lean back and close my eyes. "Did he say anything about you?"

"Oh, yes." She nods excitedly. "He said that you guys should take me to Disney World," she says proudly. "And he told me that I am the best person in the whole wide world." Wyatt and I both chuckle, hugging our daughter as the sky shifts to a cotton candy pink.

The best choice I ever made in my life was to look up into caramel-colored eyes.

This is the life I never imagined I could have; with the man I never saw coming.

And now I'm surrounded by wildflowers everywhere I go.

Scout's Cinnamon Pancake Recipe

CINNAMON PANCAKES

1 1/2 cups (195 grams) all-purpose flour

1 tablespoon brown sugar

1 tablespoon baking powder

1 tablespoon ground cinnamon

1/2 teaspoon kosher salt

1 1/4 cups (295 ml) milk

1 large egg

3 tablespoons butter, melted

1 teaspoon vanilla extract

1/4 cup chopped pecans, optional

CREAM CHEESE GLAZE

4 tablespoons butter

3 ounces cream cheese

1 1/2 cups (170 grams) powdered sugar, sifted

1/2 teaspoon vanilla extract

3 to 4 tablespoons milk

MAKE PANCAKES

1. In a large bowl, whisk together flour, sugar, baking powder, cinnamon, and salt.

2. In a medium bowl, whisk together milk, egg, melted butter, and one teaspoon of vanilla extract.

3. Heat a large skillet or griddle over medium heat. You know when the pan is ready if, when you splatter a little water onto the pan surface, the water dances around the pan and eventually evaporates.

4. Make a well in the center of the flour mixture, pour in the milk mixture, and stir the two mixtures until combined. It's okay if the batter has small lumps, in fact you want that—it is important not to over-stir the batter. Don't be surprised if the pancake batter bubbles a bit, it's normal.

5. Lightly spray skillet or griddle with non-stick cooking spray or lightly brush with melted butter. Then use a 1/4-cup measuring cup to spoon batter on to the skillet or griddle. Gently spread the batter into a 4-inch circle. The batter will be quite thick.

6. When you begin to notice the edges of the pancake look dry and little bubbles start to appear on the top surfaces of the pancake, turn over. This takes about 2 minutes. Once flipped, cook another 1 to 2 minutes or until lightly browned and cooked in the middle.

MAKE GLAZE

1. Melt butter in a small saucepan over medium heat. Remove pan from heat then whisk in the cream cheese. It will look separated at first, but after whisking it will come together into a thick paste. Whisk in the powdered sugar, vanilla extract, and 2 tablespoons of the milk. You

want to be able to drizzle the glaze over the pancakes. If it's too thick, add another tablespoon or two of milk.

TO FINISH: Serve warm pancakes drizzled with the glaze.

Stay Tuned

UP NEXT: CHANGE ME UP

S tay tuned for Book Three of The Foundation Series.

Change Me Up follows interior designer Paige Russo and Rhys Burke, CEO, on their unexpected journey of love and growth. And it all starts with an eye roll and a taco shirt.

This book has

- ADHD & anxiety representation

- "He's sort of my boss" vibes

- Artsy free spirit vs reformed playboy CEO

- Opposites attract

- Instant attraction

- Dual POV

Acknowledgements

To my Grandma—my own personal Scout. Spending time with you brought forth some of my favorite memories, whether it was watching *Young and the Restless*, doing the Irish Jig, or playing cards with you, you made every part of me shine brighter. Losing you broke me in more ways than anyone could have ever known. August sixth has been a day of sadness and pain every year since 2013, so I'm hoping this book can honor you. That every year I can be reminded of how much you shaped my life. You were my compass without even knowing it. I find you in the subtle moments of life: a cup of tea, a sunset, the stars. But now, with every flower Thomas brings me, every plant that we admire, I find you there too.

Thomas, *you are the best person in the world*. I'd love to think that Whitney and Wyatt's Thomas will love nature, dinosaurs, and tractors as much as you do, and that he fills their days with as many hugs and compliments as you do for us. You healed so many parts of me; you have no idea how lucky I am to be your mom. Never lose your ability to brighten people's days and never, ever stop finding beauty in dandelions.

To my own version of Wyatt, the man who has loved me through the worst versions of myself; the man who made me feel loveable. The one who healed me time and time again and has fought for me to know *and* feel my worth. **You unbroke me**. I am so glad that we found each other in this great big world. I love you forever.

To my best friend, my April *and* Ellie. *My found family.* The person who has picked me up when I was down more times than I can count, thank you for always showing up for me and loving me—especially while I navigated the loss of my grandma. I probably owe you for all the free therapy you've given me and the nine thousand hours of voice notes/videos you've received over the years. I love you always, Ani bananie, broom and all.

My Alphabet Soup Group and my Beta Fish, I'm not sorry for how many of you cried while reading through the document, that was kind of the goal! As always, thank you for keeping the comments unhinged, giving me a laugh, and helping to elevate my story. I'll work on writing the Wyatt and Grant bromance book for you some day! Thank you for your feedback, but most of all, thank you for all the love and support. **I love you all fiercely!**

Cait and Chelsey, my editor duo team, thank you for reading this story and for helping me ensure Whitney and Wyatt's voices relate to my readers. Thank you for seeing my vision and helping me bring it to life. It was truly a pleasure to work with you both on this story. For the record, I'm proud of you too.

To my readers, I'll probably say this about every book I write, but this one was very personal for me. I hope that anyone who has dealt with loss, abuse, or difficult relationships was able to find some peace in this novel. *You are not alone.* And in case you don't hear it enough, you *are* good enough, and you deserve a happy ending to your story.

Thank you for reading my stories and taking this journey with Whitney and Wyatt . . . and me! I cannot wait for you to meet Rhys and Paige next.

About The Author

C aitlin Klassen is a stay-at-home mom, romance writer, and loving wife. Although this book is set in the US, she was born and raised in Canada, and currently lives in a small town on the outskirts of Ottawa, ON.

Writing and books have been a safe haven for her since she was a kid, using journaling, poetry, short stories and novels, as a way of creativity. She published her first novel *The Write Kind of Temptation* in December 2023 and has no plans to stop writing books that ground you and make you feel seen.

Stay tuned for the rest of The Foundation Series: *Change Me Up* and *Fix Me Up* coming out in 2024 & 2025.

Out Now

The Foundation Series:

Book One: *From The Ground Up*

Book Two: *Build Me Up*

Other Works:

The Write Kind of Temptation

Follow her to stay up-to-date on her writing journey:

Instagram: @authorcaitlinklassen

Goodreads: goodreads.com/authorcaitlinklassen

For business inquiries only:

Email: authorcaitlinklassen@gmail.com

Milton Keynes UK
Ingram Content Group UK Ltd.
UKHW021020290724
446271UK00015B/756

9 798227 783820